THE HUSSAR

Also by DAVID R. SLAVITT

POETRY

The Tristia of Ovid
The Walls of Thebes
The Elegies to Delia of Albius Tibullus
Big Nose
Dozens
Rounding the Horn
Vital Signs: New and Selected Poems
The Eclogues and the Georgics of Virgil
Child's Play
The Eclogues of Virgil
Day Sailing
The Carnivore
Suits for the Dead

FICTION

The Agent, with Bill Adler
Alice at 80
Ringer
Cold Comfort
Jo Stern
King of Hearts
The Killing of the King
The Outer Mongolian
ABCD
Anagrams
Feel Free
Rochelle, or Virtue Rewarded

NONFICTION

Observing Physicians
Understanding Social Psychology,
   with Paul Secord and Carl Backman

EDITOR

Land of Superior Mirages:
   New and Selected Poems of Adrien Stoutenberg

THE HUSSAR

A Novel by DAVID R. SLAVITT

Louisiana State University Press
Baton Rouge and London

Designer: Albert Crochet
Typeface: Linotron Trump
Typesetter: G&S Typesetters, Inc.
Printer: Thomson-Shore, Inc.
Binder: John H. Dekker & Sons, Inc.

10 9 8 7 6 5 4 3 2 1

Library of Congress Cataloging-in-Publication Data

Slavitt, David R., 1935–
    The hussar.

    "My version of Theodor Fontane's novel: A Man of
honor"—Foreword.
    I. Fontane, Theodor, 1819–1898. Schach von
Wuthenow.   II. Title
PS3569.L3H8   1987   813'.54   86-21378
ISBN 0-8071-1364-6

For Leslie Phillabaum
with gratitude
and in friendship

CONTENTS

Foreword   ix

PART ONE

    I • *The Lieutenant*   3

    II • *Wanda*   7

    III • *Officers' Mess*   13

    IV • *Captain Kraus*   17

    V • *The Batman*   21

    VI • *Moving In*   24

    VII • *The Plan*   29

    VIII • *The Poison*   33

    IX • *The Legacy*   39

    X • *The Declaration*   42

    XI • *Seduction*   48

    XII • *Destiny*   57

    XIII • *Advice*   60

    XIV • *Review*   66

    XV • *The Feint*   70

    XVI • *The Impostors*   77

    XVII • *Words Made Flesh*   83

    XVIII • *An Understanding*   86

PART TWO

    XIX • *At the Limits of Fantasy*   99

    XX • *Brandy or Port*   104

XXI • *An Honest Involvement*   106

XXII • *A Simple Suggestion*   110

XXIII • *A Correction and an Invitation*   113

XXIV • *Old Acquaintance*   121

XXV • *Wanda Confides*   125

XXVI • *The Rewards of Gallantry*   130

XXVII • *A Lure*   136

XXVIII • *The Dream Come True*   141

XXIX • *Maneuver*   145

XXX • *Jeu de Cartes*   150

XXXI • *Rite of Passage*   157

XXXII • *Notes*   164

PART THREE

XXXIII • *A Chance Meeting*   169

XXXIV • *The Last Word*   175

Foreword

The Hussar is the result of a kind of literary parlor game—although a game played in deadly earnest that sustained me at a particularly difficult time in my life.

It is, in fact, my version of Theodor Fontane's novel, *A Man of Honor*, a book I had not read but a description of which I had come across in an essay by Gabriele Annan in *The New York Review* (of October 2, 1982). This essay on the nineteenth-century Prussian novelist who is best known for *Effi Briest*, discussed several other works of his, and it had to rely on plot summaries because not even the readers of that publication were likely to be familiar with Fontane's writings. I was intrigued by the brief outline of the story of a *ménage à trois*, of innocence and realism, and of honor and violence—a story that seemed to me easier to tell now than it would have been in 1883 when Fontane set about it.

My thought then was that it would be fun to try to write the book and, when I was finished, to go to the library and get E. M. Valk's translation of Fontane's version. I could see how I had done in comparison.

How I fared is a question that must, of course, be left to the reader to decide. My own view is implied, I think, by my decision to publish and by my sincere invitation here to those who are sufficiently curious to go and consult the earlier volume. On the other hand, it ought also to be made clear that the story I am telling here is Fontane's story, and that there is obviously an act of homage in any such retelling of another man's tale.

D. R. S.

PART ONE

I · *The Lieutenant*

It was a town of no significance. One might have passed through it in a coach-and-four and hardly noticed it except as an instant's respite from the green blur of the surrounding woods or the brown of tilled fields. It offered nothing of interest to prompt an inquiry of one's coachman, "Where are we?"

A crossroads to begin with, it had grown into a small market village that had attracted a few artisans. But then, in the conference room of some faraway palace or other, diplomats had traced an arbitrary line with a dead cigar upon one of the large-scale maps before them on the green baize table and what had been Waldenburg became Walbrzych. Or the transformation might have gone the other way.

There was a barracks in the town; handsome young officers of one or another of the great European powers gave way to a different regiment with new uniforms and a new translation of the same old standing orders. The two taverns in the town continued to do good business and the mute blacksmith kept on shoeing the officers' horses, which spoke neither German nor Hungarian nor Polish.

It was the custom followed alike by Germans, Austrians, Hungarians, and Poles to keep the men in the barracks but to billet officers in the houses in town, the best and grandest for the commander, and then downward in size and location according to the ranks, majors and captains in the villas just to the north and east of town and lieutenants farther out in the modest but still comfortable farmhouses within easy ride of the barracks. These arrangements were so obvious as to be perhaps inevitable, but in the flat planes of most generalizations there are often some idiosyncratic wrinkles. In the simple logistical business here, one of those families in town remembered some connection-by-marriage to the wife of Count Haugwitz, whose influence with the general staff was considerable. Letters were exchanged, words spoken, orders dispatched, and the billeting assignments were redone. One major moved out, restoring his unwilling host and hostess to the privacy their tenuous connection with the count had earned them. The captains had to move down the scale, and the lieutenants were then similarly displaced. Finally, Lieutenant Stefan F——, the regiment's most junior officer, found himself assigned to the farmhouse of a certain Sonja Krasinska, a widow, who lived on the north road with a daughter, Eugenie.

This young lieutenant of hussars had joined the regiment only recently. A handsome fellow, he looked all the more impressive in the fawn britches, the blue coat with the gold epaulets, the gold-buttoned undertunic, and the tall shako with the black plume that constituted the uniform of the regiment. His hip-high black boots shone with a high gloss, partly because they were new and partly because his orderly had gone over them with a soft brush not an hour ago. Stefan delighted in his appearance, of which he was acutely conscious. The look of his boots against the white flanks of his horse seemed to confirm all that he had worked for and dreamed of. He could actually look down and see his achieved status in the world. He could listen to the iterative praises of the slap of his scabbard against the leather of his saddle or the chink of his spurs as he trotted down the country road in a slanting afternoon light that sliced through the foliage of overarching trees. He accepted as the right resonance of his being this altogether agreeable frame for the wonderful picture he knew he made, and he speculated about this widow—to whom he would be respectful, almost apologetic, because he could, with his commandant's warrant in

4

his pocket, afford to be elegantly polite. Of course, on her part, she would be appreciative of his delicacy and happy to have so distinguished a guest in her home. He could already imagine evenings of whist with glasses of hot tea from a bright samovar, all the comforts of home even out here in this remote border town.

Silly? Vain? Yes, of course, but it was not altogether the young man's fault. Or, if it was his fault, it wasn't one for which he was solely responsible. He had lived up until this moment a rather dreary life, not so much physically deprived as with a metaphysical insubstantiality—or, anyway, that sense that everything about him, his classmates, school books, furniture, the very horsehair mattress on which he slept under the eaves of his uncle's house had been temporary and would soon give way to his real life, the exercise and enjoyment of his true being. He had for so long deferred his hopes that there was now a wonderment that seemed to light up the most ordinary events. He put on his uniform and then had to glance in the mirror to confirm that his was the face under the shako. He mounted his white gelding, caught a glimpse of his reflection in a shopkeeper's window, and felt . . . almost a relief to have it established that he was not still dreaming. For so long had he lived in the future that the present was a bauble of an intricacy and fragile delicacy he feared might shatter. He still dreaded the bleakness he had known all his life and to which he had always returned even after the most vivid daydreams and fantasies.

So, yes, there was vanity, but there was nothing vicious in it, nothing flighty. He wanted only to wear the uniform proudly and bring honor to it. He even understood that there was something a little less than perfectly chivalric in the way he reveled in his rank, his uniform, and the smell and squeak of its highly polished leather. But he knew, too, that it was to this very weakness that the colonel had appealed when he had made the speech welcoming the newly commissioned officers, urging them to live up to the splendor of their new plumes and swords, the brightness of which was nothing compared to the brightness of the regiment's glory. Even the older officers seemed to stand just a little taller, listening to these inspiring words.

There would come a time, he supposed, when he would be tested and his pretensions would be tried in the fires of experience and found to be the precious metal of truth or the dross of lip service and convention. He was therefore and to that extent still living in the future, waiting for his time to come. But he was approaching it. With every step his horse took upon this almost submarine passageway beneath the arching branches, he was drawing closer to his time of trial. With every tick of the pocket watch he wore, a bequest from his late father, it was looming nearer. He expected it to be on a battlefield with bullets flying and the cries of the wounded sounding piteously in his ears. He rather supposed it might have something to do with the saving of the regimental colors, which he could almost feel himself snatching up before they touched the churned-up ground.

Never for a moment did it cross his mind that these times of trial can sneak up on a fellow, can lie in wait to ambush him from behind an innocent hayrick on a quiet afternoon in the countryside, or can lurk in the coziness of a country farmhouse, where a widow lives with her daughter, a little way out of town on the north road.

II · *Wanda*

On the veranda, Stefan raised his hand to turn the polished brass handle of the mechanical bell but then hesitated so he could enjoy the instant of anticipation. Would the widow be young and beautiful, still perhaps in mourning but just about to blossom forth all the more luxuriantly, like a pruned bush that blooms again in greater profusion than before it was cut back? Why not? Would his gentle reserve, his exquisite balance of military courtesy and personal charm be exactly what she needed to be drawn forth once again into the colors and textures of living? He saw her as dark haired, pale, slender, graceful, with perfectly arched eyebrows and a high smooth forehead.

Now, why on earth not? He knew he was indulging himself, but of all the ways that she might be, that certainly was one of them, no more or less likely than any other. The baby? A sickly infant, a nonentity. It might even die, so that he could console her. Or it might recover because he rode out at night at a full gallop to fetch its medicine from town. And she would be so grateful, so very appreciative. The child, now that he thought of it, would love him at once, would march about, playing soldier. He might buy it a little hat just like his own and a toy sword. Or, wait, wasn't the child a daughter?

All this appeared, as it can to the young, in a blink of the eye. Possibilities swam on the surface of a world as bright and smooth as that of the brass handle, which he twirled, producing a muffled ringing within. Eager to see how the fact would follow upon the fantasy, obediently or in mockery (and if in mockery, gentle or cruel), he rang a second time. Then he retreated half a step and drew himself almost to attention. He wanted to impress but not to frighten.

"Yah?"

His bubble burst. He had to fight to keep his smile within civil limits and hope it might still be interpreted as mere geniality. A crone had opened the door. She had a nose that hooked downward and a chin that hooked upward, so that it seemed only a matter of time before they would meet, the pincers in a textbook attack. Her steely hair was pulled straight back and fastened in a bun. She was short and round but there was something birdlike in the way she held her head cocked to one side and peered aslant.

"Frau Krasinska?" the lieutenant of hussars asked.

"Who is asking?"

He gave his name and title. Of course, this was not Frau Krasinska but a servant, a faithful family retainer toward whom Stefan could now afford generosity as she spun out toward the periphery of his attention. He could even acknowledge that she had not always looked like this and grant her a season of plump peasant beauty and flirtatious gaiety. No doubt, he would be hearing the barely audible sounds of her humming of old love songs as the poor dear skated about the hardwood floors with her feet swathed in polishing rags.

"You will come inside?" she asked, apparently for the second time.

"Oh, yes, thank you."

"I call the lady."

He waited in the foyer. There were large botanical prints showing the leaves and seeds of various kinds of herbs and household plants and giving their names in Latin, German, French, Polish, and Hungarian. A small pewter chandelier graced the hallway. The matching arches, to left and right, gave on to a formal parlor and a less formal living room. Frau Krasinska was in the latter room, seated on a sofa with a needlework frame before her. A fire crackled in the fireplace. "Welcome, lieutenant," the woman said, and then, to the servant, "Thank you, Wanda. That will be all."

"I'm sorry to impose upon you this way," Stefan began. It was the sentence he had rehearsed for himself.

"We're happy to have you here," she said. "There is room. And in these terrible times, to have a man about the house is a comfort."

The room was rather crowded, almost fussy, filled with furniture and then liberally strewn with knickknacks on every available horizontal surface. On the walls, there were paintings, silhouettes, pressed flowers, and sconces. The upholstered chairs and plush sofas were scattered with pillows with needlework covers and silk or cloth-of-gold tassels. And Frau Krasinska? She, too, seemed just a bit overstuffed, with her plump cheeks, her pudgy hands and ample bosom decorated with a number of rings and brooches. A pair of dangling earrings glittered as she moved her head. She wore a filigreed silver comb and she peered at her guest through a bejeweled lorgnette. She seemed to be forty, or perhaps forty-five.

Stefan accepted her invitation to be seated. He found himself revising the arithmetic upon which he had based his projections. It was like a problem in trajectories that a gunnery officer might have to solve. If the widow was forty-ish, then her daughter might be twenty-ish, which might be agreeable. Risky, too, but life is full of risks. It is not in the nature of an officer of hussars to shun peril or flinch from danger.

"A cup of tea?" Frau Krasinska offered. "The samovar is still hot."

He accepted with a self-conscious grace, trying not to startle at the one accurate detail of his earlier imaginings. The domestic comforts he had envisioned had been epitomized by a samovar, even though this was not the region in which one would expect to find such things. The countryside here varied in its tastes and allegiances, and its people aped different capitals almost at random, with their heavy tea-services *à l'anglaise* or little coffee cups *à la turque*. A samovar with its hearty Muscovite cheer was less likely, but he had got that part of it right. Would the daughter, then, be beautiful, impressionable, and almost too eager to give her heart to the handsome young officer, so that he would have to exchange roles with her and play the retiring quarry to her ardent pursuer? Would she look like her mother, with that same impressive bosom he had been admiring? (Quite possibly it was a family trait to be so gorgeously endowed. Why not, why not? he almost pleaded.)

She was still welcoming him, offering whatever she could in the way of service and apologizing for Wanda's shortcomings. Wanda, he remembered, was that reverend beldam who had admitted him. An old family retainer, Frau Krasinska was explaining, less agile than heretofore but not to be cast aside on that account.

"Certainly not," Stefan agreed, explaining that his own orderly would be looking after him, doing his laundry and polishing his boots. Actually, he would be taking most of his meals at the officers' mess. A morning cup of coffee or tea, and neither the madame nor Wanda would be troubled any further. He'd disappear and return only in the late evening. He'd see to his horse and retire to his room. "Madame, I promise you, you'll hardly notice that I'm here."

"That's very good of you. But surely on the weekends? You will have a free day from time to time? It must be lonely so far from home. We wish to make you comfortable, to take you into our home in spirit as well as in physical fact. Anything less would be demeaning to both parties."

"You are very kind," he said.

There had been no mention yet of a daughter. He was waiting. Had he heard it wrong, back at the barracks? Had they been teasing him? Or was there really a daughter, who had been sent hurriedly away to visit some distant cousin in a nearby town?

Even that distressing possibility (or likelihood? or almost inevitability? The more he considered it, the more he felt persuaded that, in this woman's place, that's exactly what he'd have done to protect his daughter.) had a flattering quality to it. At least it acknowledged the danger of his presence, his theoretical seductiveness, or her susceptibility to the curl of a mustachio and the deep rumble of a masculine laugh. Perhaps, as he came to be a more and more familiar fixture and earned the widow's trust, she might allow her daughter the treat of a visit home?

A door banged somewhere in the rear of the house. "That will be my daughter, Eugenie," the frau told him, proving him wrong again.

He refused to allow his hopes to soar too high. He forced himself to imagine a dumpy young thing with a moustache, a squint, a snaggletooth that might suggest a unicorn's horn, and a pockmarked complexion. This was just a billet. He had no right to expect romantic intrigue as well. The fictions of barracks stories and the scarcely more refined gossip of the officers' mess not withstanding, some woeful creature would surely appear . . .

But she was altogether lovely. She had been out in the woods, gathering mushrooms, and had a full basket on her arm for her mother's inspection. She turned the corner, appeared in the archway that communicated from living room to hallway, and suddenly, beautifully froze. He noticed eyes of a deep deep blue no sensible painter would dare. He saw— and all but felt—her slender waist. She had long shiny blond hair that was tied behind her head with a slip of blue silk ribbon and then allowed to cascade carelessly down her back. A sharply defined, delicately sculpted nose with the flanges of the nostrils rising slightly suggested (it was difficult to say why) intelligence.

"Mama?"

"This is the lieutenant," Frau Krasinska told her.

Stefan set his teacup down on the small end table and stood, coming stiffly to attention. "How do you do?"

"My daughter, Eugenie," the widow said, completing the formula. He could not quite make out her tone. Apologetic? Wistful? Had the mother perhaps entertained the fleeting wish that she and her daughter might somehow reverse their roles? What a beautiful girl, or young woman, or, no, still a girl!

"How do you do?" Eugenie said.

And then she took a couple of steps forward to show her mother the mushrooms she had gathered. The lieutenant was not quite sure, but as he watched he saw the slight jerkiness repeat itself. There was something wrong with her foot. He understood the mother's tone, its wistfulness and pity. The girl was lame.

He looked away, pretending to gaze out the window at a prospect of kitchen garden and green lawn with the dark trunks of trees lined up in formation just beyond. He saw Wanda bearing across the lawn, not quite running but moving very fast, in pursuit, he realized, of a chicken for the evening's meal. As she turned, following the fowl's erratic flight, Stefan saw a glint of light from the blade of her huge butcher knife. It gleamed like the sword of an officer on parade.

In an opera or a ghost story, it would have been an omen.

"Would you care for some tea, my dear?"

"No, thank you, Mama," the daughter answered. "Lieutenant, a pleasure."

"The pleasure is entirely mine," he said.

He watched her try to conceal her limp as she retired from their company.

III · *Officers' Mess*

There was an elaborate chandelier hanging from the center of the room in which the officers took their meals. In the afternoons little rainbows swam along the walls, the progeny of sunbeams and the dangling prisms of crystal. The chandelier was a luxury, as were the crystal decanters and the silver epergne that graced the center of the table below it, but the tradition of the hussars was to indulge in luxury. Who deserved it more? The good things in life were theirs for the taking, were the very least they ought to be able to expect in exchange for having put their lives at risk for king and country.

In point of fact, the risk was not so great. The regiment had suffered few fatalities within the memory of even the oldest veteran and none of these had been in combat. There had been a neck broken in a steeplechase ride across rough country, and one suffered in a fall from a rooftop where some drunken officers were practicing their scaling techniques, but these were more the perils of youth than of military service. Still, the tradition was there and the assumption of a willingness to undergo the risk of combat should the need ever actually present itself. It was always a possibility that they might be ordered, on the morrow, into their formations, onto the field of battle, and up some heavily defended hill. With whatever private misgivings, they'd have gone, some of them even smiling gallantly and encouraging their brother officers and their men.

For that willingness, did they not deserve something? The

13

question, in rather less abstract form, was what they discussed endlessly beneath the warm lights of the chandelier they'd carried with them from their latest posting, along with the china, the silver, the showy epergne, the delicate *salières*, and the colonel's resplendent Turkish carpet. These were all badges of merit as precious as those they wore upon their tunics. Proud of them, the hussars felt a kind of obligation to live up to them—which is why the colonel permitted and even encouraged such indulgences.

The consolations extended beyond such *objets de vertu* to horses, pipes, cigars, boots, wines, brandies, and, of course, women. Most of all, women—because all the others were available to anyone with refined tastes and a full purse. But women, the adoration of women, the availability of all kinds of women from girls in the streets to dowager countesses, the enjoyment of women . . . therein lay their particular distinction. Do you find a civil servant carousing in taverns? Do you see him climbing down trellises, or hear him singing sentimental songs late at night in the parlors of the more fashionable bagnios of the capital? No, it isn't a part of his folklore. He may, indeed, indulge, but he does so discreetly, almost furtively, always worried lest he see his *chef de bureau* or deputy minister and lose his place. Similarly, the physician, the attorney, the professor, the tradesman, and the artisan will find themselves companionship, but without the bravura.

For Stefan, this was an exhilarating new set of principles and ideas. He had been listening to the talk of his companions for some weeks now, and had drunk it all in with the *eau de vie* that they were favoring that season. His stern uncle seemed impossibly out of date and very far away. Surely, Uncle Otto had been "laboring under a misapprehension" (which was what Uncle Otto said when he meant "wrong"). The officers, it turned out, all knew people like Uncle Otto, and what united them was their contempt for the Uncle Ottos of this world. Hussars, they had a different standard, a higher and truer notion of honor.

On his way back into town, Stefan thought of Uncle Otto

14

and Aunt Mathilde, the people who had raised him from boyhood. His own parents had been killed in an avalanche on the trip they'd taken to celebrate their twelfth wedding anniversary. A late spring storm in the Tyrol had swept them away and left Stefan an orphan, to be cared for by his mother's older brother Otto, an inspector of weights and measures in the municipal government of the capital city. Through his connection with the minister of interior, Otto had been able to arrange the appointment of his nephew to the regiment of hussars, even though this was a peculiar thing for him to have done. Stefan understood quite well that Uncle Otto disapproved of the hussars as strongly as any of the hussars disapproved of people like him. Still, there had been an obligation, a favor Uncle Otto had convinced himself that the minister owed him, a debt it was Otto's right (and, therefore, duty) to collect.

Stefan felt an almost lordly compassion for poor, dear Uncle Otto—who was neither poor nor dear and would have resented most bitterly any such imputation. Stefan could afford to think kindly of his uncle, now that he was beyond the reach of the man's authority and discipline. But what had brought his uncle and aunt to mind was the thought that Frau Krasinska and her daughter seemed much closer to the world of Otto and Mathilde than to that of the officers' mess. Abandoned temptresses and provocative maidens coiled through the evening's talk, with the sinuosity of cigar smoke billowing up into the candlelight, but they faded away just as quickly into insubstantial air. It was puzzling.

He decided, during the course of his return journey, that the most prudent thing would be to say little. He would wait upon *events*, as Uncle Otto used to advise. He dismounted and gave his horse into the groom's care.

In the officers' mess, one of the captains asked him about his billet.

"It appears quite comfortable," Stefan said.

"And with whom will you be living?" the captain asked quite innocently.

"A widow. And her daughter."

"Ah, yes? And how did they strike you?" he pressed on.

"Quite . . . decent," Stefan said. The word had leapt to his tongue unbidden.

"Too bad," said one of the lieutenants.

"But cheer up, my lad," the captain said. "It's early days yet. Your first impression may not be your last. There's always hope for a hussar!"

"Good-looking, at least?" the lieutenant asked.

"Decent," Stefan said, stuck with that word.

It provoked a laugh.

IV · *Captain Kraus*

I was, I am, I confess, that captain.

I ought to introduce myself. I am Captain Rudolph Kraus, which is misleading because my father was almost certainly not Franz Kraus, Councillor of State, but General Friedrich Leinsdorf, chief of staff of the imperial army and my patron and benefactor. My mother was Theresa Hubner Kraus, whose mother had been mistress to Ferdinand I, the Hapsburg emperor of Austria-Hungary who abdicated in 1848. I set this down with neither pride nor particular regret. When I was younger, it used to bother me, these vagaries of fate, the fact that my destiny had nothing whatever to do with my own talents or efforts but had been settled well in advance of my birth by these arbitrary considerations. Noble blood flows in my veins and yet I am not noble. Neither am I a commoner, with the ambition, the dedication, and, above all, the belief in hard work that will surely be rewarded in the long run as I improve my lot in the world. I know how fate lurks in the turn of a card or of an ankle, or even in the look of a village in the twilight that prompts a crown prince to decide it might be well to stop here for the night on the way to his hunting lodge, for the sky after all is threatening and the inn seems to be comfortable . . .

The Greeks understood these matters, admitting that their destinies were largely influenced by the carryings-on of gods who were spoiled, self-indulgent, and even rather silly—the very gods a philosopher, looking at the workings of this world, might infer. The democracies miss the point. They insist on serious gods, want to get rid of their frivolous aristocrats, and then are distressed that they have no one left but themselves to blame for the mess of things. The mess seems always to persist, in all nations, at all times, and under all systems. The only question is how to accept it cheerfully, or assign blame for it far enough away or high enough up as to allow most men and women to get on with the business of their lives.

The crown prince found the daughter of the innkeeper attractive. She was my grandmother, a young girl then, and not yet the great beauty of her generation. But a fair degree of her reputation as a beauty was a consequence of the length and distinction of her list of lovers. Toward the end of her career, she was still a magnet, but by then her attractive powers were no longer those of free-floating lust. So well connected was she with so many distinguished gentlemen that she had influence to peddle, could arrange meetings, ask favors, and contrive little dinner parties to which no gentleman could refuse an invitation. She therefore could help her protégés, who now came to pay her court with an even greater fervor than had their predecessors, ever since Ferdinand's roving eye had settled, for a moment, for the evening, upon her round scrubbed face.

I like to imagine her parents, and how they must have been so exquisitely balanced between their burgher's morality and greed, their eagerness for all the good things that might come from this association and fear of all the bad things that could just as easily arise. They had no idea what the specifics were or what the odds might be in either category. Their daughter was, in any event, extraordinarily lucky. First of all, it was clear that she was a virgin. And, second, she happened to conceive—my mother's elder brother, who later became Count von Neumann. That piece of beginner's luck in the gynecological sweepstakes won her a place at least for a time as *maîtresse en titre*—with an apartment in Vienna, a maid, a butler, and even a blackamoor to open the door and to serve coffee. I have seen a painting of my grandmother that shows the blackamoor decked out in a turban with a plume and a large, presumably glass jewel making a third eye in the middle of his forehead. My mother, Theresa Hubner, was brought into the world two years later. She remained Theresa Hubner, was never ennobled, was never cultivated as a connection to the imperial family. The revolution of 1848 intervened, and when Ferdinand abdicated in favor of his nephew, Franz Josef, our credentials, never very good to begin with, were somewhat devalued. Still, I am a bastard member of one of the great ruling houses of Europe. And more than anything that has happened to me, more than anything I have done or failed to do, that fact has influenced me, coloring the skies of my existence.

My grandmother set up a kind of salon and managed to flourish, trafficking in offices and appointments, acting as a broker for the perquisites of money and power, finding a place in some bureau for a dull younger son, locating a suitable apartment for a temporary mistress, or negotiating a loan from time to time for an embarrassed nobleman. Her accomplishments were subtle but considerable, and among them I suppose I must mention her arrangement of the marriage of her daughter, Theresa, to Councillor of State Franz Kraus, whose name I bear, and whose blood almost certainly flows in the veins of my elder brother Erwin. She may, at a later time, have introduced my mother to General Leinsdorf, who may or may not be my father but who certainly must consider himself at least a candidate for that honor. Nothing has ever been demanded of him, of course, but the goodness of his heart has been such that he has looked after me, keeping a fond eye on my progress, pleased that I have managed, at least so far, to avoid ruin.

I go into these details of my background, as I say, not out of vainglorious fascination with how the universe contrived to produce so extraordinary a fellow as myself but because the bower of bliss of which Stefan has now crossed the threshold was not altogether unlike my own mother's and grandmother's situation. What was so entrancing to Stefan—unimaginably glamorous, hypnotic, exquisite, and, as we shall see, ruinous—would have seemed to them and to me, too, quite unremarkable. This is how people live. This is, in particular, how women often manage to live, being agreeable however they can in order to gain whatever security and protection their associations in the world can afford. They are not such mysterious or ethereal creatures. Their motives are generally the obvious ones, and their methods are relatively straightforward, to use whatever they have in whatever manner seems most advantageous or least risky.

This is not a spicy story, *messieurs-dames.* On the contrary, it is very sad, farcical perhaps, but sad, as we may expect with innocence as it blunders into the pitfalls and pratfalls of the real world. Stefan was an innocent, but not a fool. He believed. He sweated and froze; he felt the breath catch in his throat and the heart pound in his chest; he experienced the delicious turning of the muscles behind his knees to jelly. I watched and was amused, or told myself I was amused. I was also envious. Who would not give the earth for such transports?

Even knowing the dangers?

Even so.

V · *The Batman*

It was up to Fritzl, Stefan's batman, to prepare the lieutenant's kit, but beneath the surface of that simple enough task, there lay a series of complicated negotiations that were necessarily collaborative. Stefan lounged on his camp bed and watched as the huge moon-faced corporal moved slowly but with a curious delicacy that suggested the antics of a circus bear and made the corresponding moves in their conversation. "You will be shaving yourself, sir?" Fritzl inquired mournfully.

"I expect so," Stefan told him.

Fritzl managed to restrain himself, did not actually shake his head, but still let his disapproval ooze out as he laid the shaving brush and the matched razors in their morocco case and stowed the talcs and lotions in the footlocker.

Quite clearly, Fritzl wanted to accompany the lieutenant and live in the billet where there would be more freedom for him. Failing that, if Fritzl had to stay in the barracks, he wanted it understood that it was only right that he should have less work to do. He was eager to find the most advantageous combination of freedom and leisure and to incur the least obligation of gratitude to his superior. Each decision, then, had to appear to be Stefan's own, unprompted by any consideration beyond his own private whim.

In fact, Stefan found himself letting Fritzl suggest the decisions. His orderly knew to the last detail what arrangements other officers had reached with their corporals.

"There are servants, sir?" he now inquired, under the guise of his proper concern that the lieutenant be comfortable and correctly cared for. Stefan was well aware that there were other considerations that might be floating about in the dimness of Fritzl's consciousness. He was perhaps imagining plump naughty chambermaids, laughing laundresses, complaisant cooks. He was also angling to find out in what ways he could reduce even further the list of his own duties, what responsibilities he could shift to other shoulders.

"One servant, so far as I was able to see," Stefan answered, "an old woman with a long nose and a turned-up chin."

"The mistress is better looking, I trust," It was close to the line, perhaps, but Fritzl never quite crossed over into impertinence. Or he never seemed to do so, which was the next best thing. Stefan knew that, fundamentally, Fritzl was always impertinent, that he had no reverence or respect in him anywhere, and that all his show of elaborate correctness was, therefore, a kind of running joke.

"Decent," he said again. Its ambiguity had served him well enough in the officers' mess.

"There's no such thing," Fritzl retorted. "Flesh is flesh and none of it's decent."

"Are you so sure?"

"Every lock has its key, they say."

"Yes, yes, I know," the lieutenant said, letting a little of his annoyance show.

The corporal busied himself arranging piles of linen in the footlocker. "Nevertheless," he said, after a suitable time had passed, "and as a gesture of appreciation, it might be a good thing for the lieutenant to bring along some chocolate or fresh fruit—difficult things to obtain these days. To share our privileges is only gentlemanly and . . . decent." It was only a hemidemisemiquaver of a pause, but it played on Stefan's *decent*, turning it indecent, turning the chocolate and fruit into bribes for favors, turning the widow and her poor lame daughter into tavern girls or whores. It was Fritzl's way of replying to his lieutenant's show of annoyance.

22

"A very good idea," he said, in order to blunt the force of his batman's rude suggestion. He could appear to be oblivious, but only at the risk of seeming stupid. Those were the choices.

Fritzl was far too clever to smile.

VI · *Moving In*

Stefan made his move the next evening, riding over to Frau Krasinska's at the head of a procession that included Fritzl on a roan mare and a teamster's wagon that carried the lieutenant's baggage and his gelding's fodder and tack. There was a groom who came along on the wagon to help install the horse properly. Stefan was not used to so much attention, and though he understood that it was the perquisite of his rank and uniform, he realized it might be intimidating to the widow and her daughter. He was glad he had taken his batman's advice and permitted a quantity of fresh fruit and chocolate to be included among his gear. This cumbersome military display demanded some gesture of diminution. Three men and four horses to move the armful of personal effects he was bringing along? Ridiculous!

On the other hand, the men were all experienced and efficient, and in half an hour were on their way back to the barracks, leaving Stefan to present his little *cadeaux* and offer his compliments. He repeated his promise to impose as little as possible. Frau Krasinska repeated her hope that he would feel welcome as a part of the household. Then he went up to his room.

The design of the house was simple, its fundamental pattern that of a square cut up into six rectangles. There was a bedroom in each corner, upstairs, and in the front middle there was a lavatory and toilet. The middle rear was the upstairs hallway. Stefan was in the right rear bedroom, which adjoined the widow's bedroom in the right front. Across the hallway from Stefan, at the left rear, was Eugenie. The left front room had been long ago converted to a study by the late Herr Krasinski and had been left that way, there being no need in the house for more dormitory space.

Stefan noticed himself noting these dispositions. Did he indeed share Fritzl's vulgar belief that flesh was flesh and none of it decent? Or was he simply exercising those skills in which he had recently been trained, learning what the topography held in the way of challenge and opportunity, should any emergency arise . . . a fire, perhaps, or an intruder. He lay under soft feather-filled comforters, trying to identify the faint scents of the pomanders that Wanda or the widow herself had put into the linen chest for their touch of refinement and grace. They were hardly provocative smells, neither heavily musky nor floral, but they had about them a feminine delicacy he had missed during his training and his posting to the regiment.

Indeed, had he grown up in another kind of household, he might not have been so susceptible to such little touches, might have learned to expect and accept them as ordinary invocations to beauty or at least to creature comfort. His dormer room in his uncle's house, bare and spare, had been a simple box to contain him, his obligation to keep it neat and clean being his only reason to pay it any attention at all. The little pot of dried heather that now stood on the nightstand he had dismissed as a mistake, something the women had simply failed to clear away. He could no more think it had been deliberately put there for his pleasure than he would have assumed that a bouquet of roses or camellias delivered to the front door was meant for him. But when he blew out the candle and got into bed, the subtle spices and florals of the perfumed sheets reached him, penetrating his defenses and diffidently insinuating themselves into his soul's keep.

And then? He was up, shaved, dressed, and to horse, off to the barracks early in the morning and out of their reach, back into the world of men and the life of the regiment. He had a day of paper work, exercises, and inspection of the guard posts. He took his meals, his tankard of ale, his one cigar of the day, and rode back to his billet. A little past nine in the evening, he entered the front gate, dismounted, and started to lead his horse around to the stable. But he looked up, his attention having been caught by some movement, and saw in that center window, which he now knew to be that of the bathroom, a silhouette. The way the curtain was hung, with its generous gathers, he could not tell if the shadow he saw was that of the mother or the daughter—or even that of the servant. But its sinuosity struck him and it fleshed itself, for he remembered how the soap smelled, how the towels felt, having been in that very bathroom himself. He found it impossible not to extrapolate from what he knew to glowing pink flesh, which he assigned more or less arbitrarily to Frau Krasinska. He forced himself to turn away and lead his horse into the barn.

He was annoyed with himself. What kind of person had he become, to stand there and gaze at a naked woman's shadow? Had he contracted some subtle infection from Fritzl? He could not put the blame on the corporal, but he had to admit that he found himself half speculating and half hoping Fritzl might yet prove to be correct in his view of the lives of these women. Was it even remotely possible that the mother and the daughter were willing and eager in the way that Fritzl had supposed but were unable to make the first move, constrained to rely on hints of scented linen as they waited in their demure impatience for him to demonstrate his manhood? He leaned his head upon the warm flank of the horse, feeling the heat and solidity of muscle and hide, and closed his eyes. He seemed to be wandering helplessly in some dream. He had no idea what to do. He told himself that Fritzl had never talked to these people, could not possibly know anything about them. He found himself disappointed, however, by that estimate of Fritzl's ignorance. Be fair, he told himself. The only right thing was to wait and see. And to keep scrupulously to his previously established pattern of behavior.

Not himself, but a clumsy understudy called in at the last moment, he entered the house and wished the widow a good evening. (Ah, so it was the daughter up there, clad only in a towel if at all.) He went upstairs to his room, undressed, and went into the bathroom to brush his teeth, and of course to be enveloped there by the languid and perfumed steaminess of Eugenie's bath. He permitted himself to tarry a bit before he marched back to his bedroom, hung his robe on its hook inside the door, and got into bed.

Sleep, however, was not subject to his command. He had to wait upon it and as he did so he listened to the noises of the house. The frau, downstairs, still reading, would move from time to time to poke the fire. Or had she come up? Was the noise from her bedroom? He recalled the image of the silhouette upon the curtain and he tried to blame the girl. Surely, she was aware that her shadow could be seen that way from the front of the house! Immediately, he found himself making excuses for her. The house was set back from the road, after all, and trees blocked the view of that front window from casual passersby. It had not been her fault. She was merely unused to the presence of men on her front lawn. Altogether innocent, but she was all the more desirable for that.

In such ways, predictable but nonetheless painful, he lay awake for much of the night. He heard the banging of a shutter somewhere at the back of the house. He heard someone, mother or daughter, get up during the night to go to the toilet. He lay there, his senses more and more acute as his fatigue scraped his nerves raw.

The next morning, he was up at dawn and out of the house even before Wanda had emerged from her room next to the kitchen. Bad as his situation was in the widow's house, it was no better in the barracks. He felt he was an impostor. These were not the emotions a hussar was supposed to feel. Lust-crazed and impotent, he was unable even to decide whether it was the overblown, bosomy mother or the shy and lame daughter he preferred to imagine bedding. Tired,

27

having slept badly if at all, he was irritable and realized he'd have to control his temper, which naturally made him self-conscious and awkward as he performed his not very taxing duties.

He had wanted an adventure, but this was a tribulation. The best he could hope for was a gradual hardening of his heart and spirit that would come when he achieved the sophistication of his brother officers, or the more vulgar cynicism of Fritzl. He drank more wine than was good for him and had several cordials after dinner. He was glad his horse had already learned the way back to Frau Krasinska's. Otherwise, he was sure, he'd have wound up on the steppes of central Asia, wambling in the wilderness between nausea and stupor.

VII · *The Plan*

It was not inevitable, he told himself. Sitting down at his writing table, he listed his choices. He could ask for a change in quarters and move back to the barracks. But he didn't believe in any solution so simple. Somehow word would get around of how he'd been smitten by a dumpy widow and her lame daughter. He felt bad enough without the mockery he knew would attend upon any request he might make for a change in billet.

Drink? He might be dismissed from the regiment for alcoholism, which would be a disgrace without dishonor. He might even become so persistent a drunk that Frau Krasinska herself would tell him to leave. Yes, yes, he could see a way, perilous and lengthy, but without humiliation, by which he could extricate himself from this intolerable situation. He could see himself pretending to take the first steps toward reform. All he had to do was drink heavily for a week or two; then he could announce that Frau Krasinska had asked him to leave, whether she had made any such request or not. He did not have to depend on her. She needn't even know why or how he had involved her.

He felt better. He had it within his power to control his fate. The only difficulty was that he was still queasy from the preceding night's unpremeditated overindulgence. It was a clever enough idea, perhaps, but could he carry it off? Could he plausibly act the role the scheme required? Or roles, for he had to be first a drunkard and then a reformed drunkard. Besides, he had to keep his resolution clearly in mind. His intention to leave the women had to be maintained despite the quantities of brandy he'd have to imbibe. That was the heart of the problem, for he wasn't sure he wanted to leave. He knew it was the prudent thing to do, and probably the decent thing, but he wasn't altogether convinced he could force himself actually to do it.

Why, then, go the other way. He could, if retreat seemed impracticable, try an attack. He could make advances so bold as to assure failure, in which case he could withdraw, not cravenly but out of tact, from a lofty consideration for the feelings he had heedlessly bruised. But how could he justify such behavior? How could he claim heedlessness even as he sat here and excogitated a plan by which he would make that objectionable advance? He looked down at the paper and saw the answer before him in his own hand, now embellished by a series of delicately shaded rectangles: "Drink." He could, as a drunk, forget himself, or seem to do so. It would be a way of saving his honor and that of the women of the household too.

And if, by some wild luck or improbable set of circumstances, his foray should prove more fortunate than he'd expected, the advance accepted and the proffered passion reciprocated . . . ? He could not even imagine an apodosis. He reached around with his left hand to rub the back of his neck where his taut muscles ached. He imagined the neck of Frau Krasinska, easily visible in its touching fragility because of the way she wore her hair upswept. He could see in that delicate cervical stalk the lithe girl she had once been. He wondered whether, given just the backs of their necks to examine, he would even be able to distinguish between Sonja and Eugenie. He groaned at his depravity, put away his pen, and crumpled his hopeless list into a crude ball, which he threw into the wastebasket.

He drew off his high boots and lay down on top of the bed, covering his eyes with his arm. His thoughts were as fevered and wild as ever. Give in to them, he told himself, and let them have their way. Just as long as you don't act upon them, you'll be all right. Admit them as fantasies, the result of boyish high spirits and inexperience, and endure them in patience and strength. All will be well. But even as he lay there, he realized that the mere show of drunkenness was all he needed, an excuse for any behavior for which, the next day, he could apologize—if apology turned out to be required. He could see himself staggering about, lurching, and falling upon . . . the mother? Yes, her first, because she would be less easily shocked, might perhaps be amused, but surely would be safe from any permanent injury to the delicacy of her feelings. She had been in the world, knew what beasts men could be, and had, Stefan believed, an admirable composure and self-possession.

Some weekend, perhaps, when he had had the leisure of an afternoon in her company, when they had had some hours together during which he could establish his inebriation and consequent lack of responsibility for any gross improprieties, he might simply declare his ardor, or better yet seize her in an irresistible embrace. Yes, that was the way they did these things in novels. And then, according to the novelists, the woman melted into one's arms, an image which had always seemed to him messy, however intimate.

Lying there on the bed, considering the depths to which he had sunk, the lengths to which his obsession seemed to be carrying him, and the heights of rapture to which he aspired, he fell asleep, still fully dressed. He awoke in the middle of the night, took off his clothes, and got back into bed, but now sleep avoided him, leaving him alert and aware of the utter stupidity of his efforts earlier in the evening. It didn't even deserve to be called a plan. To get drunk? To have an excuse to behave as badly as he was already inclined to do? To make plausible the claim that he was so drunk that the widow asked him to leave her house? It all now seemed preposterous. If only they knew, in their rooms next door and across the hall, how they would despise him! How contemptible they would both think him . . .

Or would they, perhaps, also find some cause for satisfaction, some degree of pleasure in his distress, however awkward, which was not without its flattery, its acknowledgment of their attractiveness. Women like to be thought of as attractive, don't they?

He stopped himself. The thought took on Fritzl's moon-faced leer and loomed in the distance, a mocking moon that presided over his disintegrating and re-forming mental landscape. By a reasonable process of association, he thought of the brighter glare of day, which surely would reveal the haggard look, the darkening circles under his eyes, the beginnings of some nervous tic that would give him away. It was only a matter of time before his obsession would be common knowledge. It wouldn't be only Fritzl but the entire regiment that would be laughing at him, the more kindly of them keeping their comments hidden from him, but all of them amused and derisive. As he would be himself, if he were to learn of some other lieutenant's ridiculous and unreciprocated passion for two entirely unsuitable females.

It was a brotherhood all right, but it had its sinister code. As in a chicken coop, any one of them, showing some blemish, some blood spot, might be pecked to death at once by the others in each of whom there would be, along with the rage and the bloodlust, more than a modicum of terror.

Another plan flashed into his mind, more dramatic than any of the earlier schemes but perhaps necessary. He could flee at once, flee not only the service but the town and the country too, take passage to America, and start over in that new land. He imagined a vast sugar plantation adjacent to a huge cattle ranch that was in turn bounded by wilderness in which gold prospectors and outlaws skirmished and savage Indians roamed in justifiable anger. He supposed he'd last no more than a matter of hours in such a place.

Good.

Eventually, there was the first brightening in the east, the signal for him to get up, take his boots, and sneak downstairs, released from his night's punishment and compelled toward the day's greater torments.

VIII · *The Poison*

The brandy, no longer part of the plan, was now merely an aid
to sleep. He had filled a large flask at the tavern and on the
way home could feel its weight in his pocket as a burden as
if, instead of mere brandy, it was the embodiment of all his
extravagant ineffectual schemes. Or the burden of his guilt.
In his distracted state, it no longer seemed a metaphor; now
it was merely and stupidly true. He felt defeat, for he knew
quite well he would not be using the brandy as an excuse for
boldness. There would be no boldness. He would just hide in
his room, taking slug after raw slug until he had attained the
insensibility he craved. It burned his hip now, much as it
would later burn his throat. He might as well have been
carrying a white flag to parley with an enemy commander
whose forces already possessed the bloody standard his own
men had allowed to be taken.

He had not yet exchanged twenty words with the women
of the house, and he understood there was no way he could
blame either of them for his undoing. He, alone, was responsible. Despite his efforts to free himself from the spell he
had cast upon himself, he was like one of those perverts who
follow women around, watching them, spying upon them,
and then, unable to bear it any longer, falling upon them
with knife or ax. Or, if Stefan had not quite reached that dangerous condition, he could understand how men got there.
He wondered whether the brandy would be helpful to him or
a danger. Strong drink, he knew, made some men merry,
others rowdy, and still others mean before they all arrived at

33

their destination of oblivion. He didn't know himself well enough to predict, but he had no reason to suppose his luck with alcohol would be any better than his luck with women. Almost certainly, he'd behave badly.

Spill it out upon the ground, then, and let it be a libation to the cruel gods? He knew he'd do no such thing. He was like an automaton, lurching along upon a ruinous course and unable to save itself. There was something almost comforting in the certainty of disaster. He sat on his horse, feeling its rocking motion at each step and watching the blurred greens at the side of the road that was familiar enough but quite new. The route seemed marked now, picked out for special attention, as any ordinary path might be if a condemned man were to tread it on his way to execution. Stefan thought of uniformed men who go off to meet their destiny in battle and the calm detachment some of the survivors claim to remember. He was able to believe it.

The weekend loomed before him. He was confident that it would be his undoing. The only open questions in his mind were how he would go down, and whether he would also destroy those around him. It was a moderately entertaining subject upon which to speculate, and he even found something soothing in its distraction as he wondered whether the regiment or the Krasinska family would soon be left devastated and resentful or delivered and grateful.

He could ride along for minutes at a time and keep his mind quite blank. But then some peculiar idea would jump out at him, attaching itself to his consciousness. He thought it was interesting, for example, that his horse, a gelding, was removed from these sordid concerns, as an Oriental guru is said to be removed from the tiresome assertion of self. The church's rule of celibacy he had always taken to be a great sacrifice on the part of the fathers and brothers and nuns, but now it seemed to him sensible and obvious. To put by all those questions of the perpetuation of the self (and what else, in the end, were love and sex for?) seemed such a comfort, even a luxury, as to be irresistibly appealing. Resign his commission then and join the church, to become a member of some contemplative order? He could make bread or take care of beehives in a remote monastery where they were used to getting up in the middle of the night. It would be rigorous and pure; there would be chanting, candlelight, and severe stone walls, cool and smooth to the touch of fevered flesh . . .

The horse turned in at the gate. Had he arrived so soon? Unprepared, he was tempted to turn and flee, spur the horse to a gallop, then fling himself off, break his neck, and extinguish at once his life and its torment. But he could not do that. All he could do was pat his flask, as the anarchist pats the bomb he carries, taking comfort in its power, security in its risk.

"Good evening," Frau Krasinska called when he had come into the house.

"Good evening," he replied, wondering how she would react if she suspected how these polite exchanges had affected him.

"You have been true to your promise," she said. "But I trust that we'll see more of you now that the weekend is here."

"I should be most happy," he said.

"You'll take your meals with us tomorrow? At the very least, you'll join us at supper?"

"Supper, yes, although I may have to go out during the day."

He looked at her, curled up on the sofa in a baby-blue crocheted shawl and with a small leather-bound volume in her hand. He could see its delicate bookmark of faded blue silk with which she kept her place. The bookmark, he realized, was the color of lingerie. Did they, in a bizarre economy, shred their worn-out camisoles and bloomers to make these bookmarks? He closed his eyes, giddy at his single-mindedness.

"You seem tired," she said, her voice rich with husky concern.

"Yes, a little."

"And here I was beginning to wonder whether you were avoiding us. I see I misjudged you. Your duties are more demanding than I had supposed."

"You're very kind," he said. "Good night." He managed to withdraw in good order and to get upstairs. He opened the flask and took a long pull at the brandy.

She was, after all, not so ravishing a creature but a quite ordinary woman, well-preserved for her age, a bit broad in the beam now and with touches of gray at the temples. She had never been a great beauty at whom men flung their hearts and fortunes. There was, however, a musky presence, a physical aura she seemed to have, but Stefan could hardly say how much his perception owed to his own admitted deprivation.

An only, lonely child, he had been orphaned and transferred to his Uncle Otto and Aunt Mathilde at the very worst moment, just at that age when the wax of a young boy's soul is most impressionably molten, in his eleventh year. He had come to know the world discontinuously and even inconsistently, remembering the warmth of his own mother and then having to face the brusqueness and cold discipline of his aunt. The idea of sex with Aunt Mathilde was so forbidding as to leave him more or less in awe of Uncle Otto, who, in Stefan's imagination, exerted himself like one of those Swiss mountaineers preparing to assault the Jungfrau. It would be a question of blind determination and fearless disregard of one's personal comfort and safety. It would have to be a commitment of an almost philosophical kind, a resolve that the thing had to be done because the very possibility was a challenge provocative in ways that Aunt Mathilde herself could never be. Stefan still associated his aunt with the smells of lye soap, carbolic cleansers, and the heavy fragrance of the lemon oil she used to rub into the dark wood furniture in her dining room.

On the one hand, there had been Aunt Mathilde and her friends, a group of women as hefty and forbidding as she. And on the other, there were the whores he passed every day on his way home from school. The implausible stories about what they did, how the sexual act was performed, and what the more inventive varieties of sexual experience might include turned out, of course, to be quite true, just as the stories he'd heard from Aunt Mathilde and Uncle Otto about storks and cabbages were false and inconsistent. The resulting alliance of the truth of the real world with the first stirrings of his own body ought to have been reassuring but wasn't. On the contrary, he felt utterly lost and beyond all hope of decency and order, qualities he still associated with the stern figures of his uncle and aunt. He knew that the combination of his own depravity and the world's would be irresistible and that it was simply a matter of time before he would be sucked down into some vortex of degradation. That was one of the reasons for his eagerness to join the regiment of hussars. The discipline, the gorgeous uniforms, the cleansing risk of death, the noble call to duty for crown and country might be antidotes to the poison, within and without, to which he knew he would otherwise surely succumb.

He lay on his bed, drinking the brandy, aware that his time of trial had at last arrived. He was curious to taste the first moments of bitterness of the lifetime of suffering and disgrace he was absolutely certain he deserved. It was not at all surprising that he had contrived to go directly to the disgrace without any intervening moments of delight and dalliance. He was unlucky as well as inexperienced, clumsy, a brute— for he had not even been able to determine in his own mind which of the females he lusted after. He had gone over the question a dozen times and had generally decided for the mother, but only because he supposed his chances of success with her were marginally greater. But when the catastrophic moment arrived, it would probably be dictated by some random circumstance of his being alone in a room with the one or the other, and his being at that instant bold or desperate enough or drunk enough. It was too stupid to contemplate, but he could think of nothing else.

He drank until the flask was empty, fell asleep, or rather, passed out, and in the morning, awoke to a brand-new experience. His head ached; his stomach was delicate; his bones seemed to have turned to glass; his mouth had been poisoned: he was hung over and felt awful. It was all he could do to get to the bathroom, drink a couple of glasses of water, empty his bladder, and stagger back to bed. He lay there, feeling the stabbing pains of the pulse in his forehead and wondering how he could possibly endure the headache and its torments when he got up, as he would soon have to do, if his stomach didn't settle, in order to return to the bathroom to vomit. He took slow, deep breaths and concentrated on riding out the waves of nausea. He imagined that he might feel better if he were to throw up, or that he might pass out—which would also be an improvement—but as long as he lay there quietly, he could suppose that Frau Krasinska and her daughter assumed he was just sleeping late. He was sure that if he tried to get up, they'd know at once not only that he was hung over but why he had drunk so much. Their peals of laughter would be like the shining blades of sharp swords cutting him right on the temple where that slash of pain was still throbbing.

IX · *The Legacy*

Do I have this right?

I confess that I am imagining a condition that is quite foreign to my own experience, which is what fascinates me about Stefan's story. He was one of those people to whom the opposite sex might as well have been inhabitants of a remote country, or indeed visitors from some distant planet. They seemed to speak a language with a recognizable vocabulary and a penetrable syntax, but they meant something altogether different, so that he felt always as though he had to translate and that he was doing it badly, getting the sense of the idioms all wrong.

But to a considerable degree, it was this very quality of being ill at ease and keyed up that I noticed and even envied. My own *éducation sentimentale* had been quite different. A bastard Hapsburg (or a Hapsburg bastard, for the operative title ought to be reserved to the end), I was nevertheless reared as a real Hubner by my mother and grandmother, both of whom believed that the influence of the church and of society in proscribing most sexual activity was exactly the contrary of what the bishops and magistrates must have intended. By forcing sex underground, those worthies made it illicit and glamorous, so that men prized it beyond its real value. It was to protect me against just the kind of susceptibility that we have seen Stefan exemplifying that they introduced me at a very early age to the lists of lust. They engaged as housemaids retired prostitutes who were no longer young enough to attract the volume of business most broth-

39

els require of their girls. Their alternatives were to go onto the streets—a dangerous and depressing comedown—or accept domestic employment in those establishments that were liberal or irregular enough to accommodate them. My grandmother found that she had her pick of a great many candidates. And part of the job, as she explained it, was to educate and amuse the young masters of the household. My brother Erwin and I were a way for them to maintain their self-esteem as professionals, and my grandmother, a clever woman, understood how that pride was important. These women were not quite yet cast out of the sisterhood.

I believe that Councillor of State Franz Kraus may even have found some benefit, himself, in these arrangements, which would in no way have displeased my mother, particularly when she was occupied with one of her charitable works—the Society for the Protection of Military Orphans, for instance—that required her to meet frequently with General Leinsdorf and took up so many of her evenings during a certain period in her life.

An unorthodox and louche ménage? Perhaps, but not so very unusual except in the openness with which we practiced the same manual of arms as other families. Drive up the long avenues between the linden trees, ascend the curving staircases, and stride through the impressive entrance halls of castles, manors, and stately homes, and you will find beyond those grandiose façades a network of servants' halls, back stairs, and curious passageways. At night, you can hear footsteps as maids and grooms run up and down, not always bearing trays of hot cocoa. All over the empire, all over Europe, and throughout the civilized world, the aristocrats are realists, willing to accept themselves for what they are because they have no need of illusion. They do not dream of anything better or different. Either because of my Hapsburg lineage or my qualification as a bastard son of a bastard daughter, I was to have that realism. It was to be my legacy.

I'd have to say, on balance, that it was an advantage, but a negative advantage. What I was saved were the agonies of puppy love, the mooncalf transports by which young boys transform altogether ordinary girls into demigoddesses, sirens, nymphs, or angels, all of which is unnecessary and rather a burden to the girls.

It is a question of economy, surely. The poor man dreams of a crust of bread or a bowl of thin soup. The rich man, whose table groans every day with the delicacies of the earth, nibbles a tidbit here and there and prays not for food but for appetite. Unlike many of my classmates in the gymnasium, I was able to see a girl or a woman as something other than the possessor of sexual organs, because I'd had the chance to accustom myself to the enjoyment of those pleasant enough toys with a series of Olgas, Marias, Catherines, Marguerites, Ilses, Wandas, Clothildes, and Cleopatras (one, I swear, insisted that her name really was Cleopatra).

What I missed was the madness, the *grande folie* that transcends the merely human, rational plane upon which we live most of the time. Transcends or falls far short. Was Stefan in a transcendent state?

I cannot decide. Perhaps it does not matter. But certainly, he was not behaving in any normal and reasonable way.

X · *The Declaration*

He may have drifted off to sleep for a while. There was no way to know, for he had no sense of time. There were instants of comparative respite but there were also periods of agony so unendurable as to make suicide seem an attractive remedy. They shoot horses, he told himself, and put them out of their misery. He wondered if one heard the report of the pistol one discharged against one's own temple. The noise would be unbearable.

Something quieter, he thought, and he considered drowning. He could fill the basin in the bathroom and quietly stick his face into the water. A moment or two of unpleasantness, hardly worse than what he was now suffering, and it would be all over, his hangover and his shameful passion with it.

There was a knock on the door. "Lieutenant? Are you ill?"

It would all be immediately revealed. He would be humiliated.

"Are you decent?" the voice called. "May I come in?"

He groaned, the door opened, and Frau Krasinska appeared, having taken his vocalization as assent. "Drink a little too much last night?" she asked, raising her eyebrows. To her, it was a joke.

Was there perhaps some hope he might not be absolutely disgraced? He managed to nod.

"What you need is more of the same."

"Oh, God! I couldn't bear it."

"It's the only cure. What were you drinking? Brandy?"

He nodded.

"A milk punch, then. You'll feel much better for it, believe me."

She went down to the kitchen to make the punch for him. He got out of bed, inched his way to the dresser, and combed his hair. Simply to stand was agony and he felt like a criminal who might at any time be discovered, but he managed to get his hair into order and himself back into bed without having been detected. He was ready for his milk punch, even though the idea of it was dreadful. He would have drunk gall or hemlock. It was a familiar kind of challenge, the swallowing down of nasty medicine. A hussar, he had his honor to maintain. When she returned, he accepted the glass and took two gulps. He hardly even made a face.

"It's odd," Frau Krasinska said. "You didn't seem so drunk when you came in last night."

"No," he agreed.

"Then you drink alone? That's very bad. A dangerous habit. Is the young lieutenant perhaps in love?"

He nodded. He had known all along that she would somehow see through him. He was afraid he was blushing.

"How wonderful for you!" she said.

He shook his head.

"There's always hope," she said, trying to raise his spirits a little. She had no idea that she was the one he was pining for. She couldn't know, could she? Had he given himself away so easily?

"Have some more," she said, picking up the pretty crystal tumbler with a pattern of leaves etched around the rim. "It will make you feel better, I promise."

He accepted the tumbler from her hand and took a sip more. He didn't feel any better yet. He was grateful not to have been nauseated by the brandy.

"A girl back in the city?" Frau Krasinska asked, seating herself on the edge of the bed as if for a cozy chat. He could have reached out and touched her thigh. He felt it pulling at the counterpane and thought of the way a magnet pulls at iron filings.

43

She had no idea she was the object of his attentions. Otherwise, she would not be here, in his bedroom, sitting on his very bed. Eugenie, who had also been a candidate, seemed to him, at that instant, pathetically thin and impossibly far away. He shook his head in reply to her question.

"Here in town then?" It was amusing to her. She was smiling. He was tempted to blurt it out, to let her know she was the one, and see her leap up from the bed as if it were burning.

"Yes," he admitted. He took another swallow of the milk punch. Now that he was confident his stomach could tolerate it, he was beginning to find it agreeable. He realized that she had grated nutmeg over the top of it. "This is very good."

"I told you."

"Won't it make me drunk again?"

"That's one of the risks. But you don't have to go to the garrison today. You're not on duty. You can be a little drunk."

"Will I be hung over again, too?"

"Not if you take it easy. Also, you have to drink lots of water. You're dried out. That's most of your problem." He nodded. He'd been right then, to drink those glasses of water. He was beginning to feel halfway human again.

"And you must eat something. That will help too," she said. "Some gruel? Or chicken soup? Which seems less revolting?"

"You're very kind," he said, wondering how often she'd been drunk and how she'd acquired all this knowledge.

As if she could read his mind, she told him, "My late husband sometimes overindulged. I learned how to take care of him."

He felt a little of his panic returning. If she could see through him that easily, how much more could she see?

"And I found it useful for myself, later on after he died. Living alone, one must sometimes drink alone, with the same unfortunate consequences." She gave him a look of commiseration that was friendly enough. He felt like a beast. If only she knew what he was thinking, or if only she looked at him and realized that beneath the counterpane he had an erection, she would get up from the bed, flee his room, leave him to suffer in his deserved and lonely torment. But she reached out and touched his stubbly chin. "A little food, another drink, some coffee, and a shave, and you'll feel almost like your old self. I promise you, the worst of it is over."

"Thank you," he said. "Perhaps, if it isn't too much trouble, I might manage a little dry toast."

"Of course. But in exchange, tell me what girl has reduced you to this sorry condition."

He blushed crimson.

"I promise, I'll keep your secret."

He shook his head, helpless. She had guessed. Or she would. It was hopeless. He had nowhere to hide.

"You won't tell me?" she asked. She cocked her head and thought. "Eugenie, perhaps?"

He nearly said it was. But he could not be untrue to Frau Krasinska. He could not be untrue to the facts of the situation as he perceived them. It would have been the coward's way to lie. "It's you," he admitted.

She laughed, then stopped laughing, and looked at him, first skeptically and then merely considering. "Me," she said, as if trying the word aloud to hear how it sounded. "You've never been with a woman, have you?"

He shook his head.

"How sweet. I'll get your toast."

It took a moment to sink in, but gradually he realized that she had not been offended, did not think him a monster, had actually smiled at him. And then she had swept away to go and make him toast.

He could scarcely believe his good fortune. The dark secret he had been hiding, even from himself, was now out in the open and . . . and nothing. She had not accepted his suit, but he had never really expected her to. He'd been so sure of the awful consequences of her learning of his lust for her that he'd barely allowed himself to consider the possibility of her welcoming such attentions. Nor did he really believe, even now, that there was any such likelihood. He was satis-

45

fied not to be punished, reported to his commander as a foul beast, sent away in disgrace, from the regiment, the town, or, most of all, the house. He was still here, apparently still welcome.

Did she not take him seriously? Did she disbelieve him? He couldn't suppose so. She had asked him about his experience with women . . .

He conceived the notion that it might amuse her to give him that experience, to take up the invitation and become whatever it was that one's first love became, not out of immediate physical desire for him or even any particular liking, but from a kind of vanity, the way people will stop to have their faces drawn by a caricaturist at a street fair, or to pose for one of those men who cuts out silhouettes, to keep an image of themselves somewhere and fight off the ravages of time. She might wish just to have her image kept, even in the memory of an unimportant hussar, flatteringly lit by desire and gratitude. Might she not return, put down the tray with the dish of toasts bundled in their napkin, step in a stately way out of her housecoat and gown, let him see for a moment the grandeur of those impressive breasts, and then blind him with them as she hugged his face to her bosom.

Almost instantly, he felt a mental reaction as part of his intelligence roused itself to make fun of his absurd and hopeless fantasies. She had hardly given any indication of acceptance. Indeed, he realized it would serve him right if she now used his confession against him, teasing him and finding ways of humiliating him. Even that would be an improvement on what had gone before, however, for it would be a relationship in which both parties actively participated. Until now, he had been like a naughty boy spying upon an unsuspecting woman from a perch in some tree, peering into her window. He remembered that silhouette framed by the bathroom window, not of Frau Krasinska but of her daughter, and realized that he had been unfaithful to the mother even before declaring his ardor. Nothing good could come of this, nothing but humiliation and suffering . . .

And yet, he felt rather better. The brandy in the milk punch had brought him considerably farther along the road to recovery than he could have hoped. And he had not shocked the woman by his confession. He told himself to be of good heart and persevere, as a hussar ought to do. He heard her steps upon the stairway and in the hall outside his door. She came back into his room with a cup of coffee and a little plate of toast.

"Have this, and then drink as much water as you can. You'll live."

"I am deeply obliged."

"I can't have you spoiling our picnic, can I?"

"Picnic?"

"Yes," she said. "I thought that you and I and Eugenie might go on a picnic this afternoon. The weather is fine. And we have a spot by the pond where we go to watch the geese. Do say you'll come."

"Yes, yes, of course. And thanks."

"Yes," she said, allowing herself a reprise of that earlier smile. "Of course you'll come. How could you refuse, after all?"

After all she had done for him? Or after all he had confessed to? Both, after all. He found himself smiling, too. It was now all amusing, amazingly pleasant and fine. He had jumped off a high building only to land on a soft pile of hay in a wagon that happened to be passing by, a piece of incredibly good luck.

It was a shame, though, that Eugenie would be coming along. He'd have preferred to be alone with Frau Krasinska. And he felt good to realize that, for it meant he had not seriously betrayed the widow, that his fancy for her daughter had been only a thing of the instant.

He ate his toast, drank his coffee, and finished the little bit of milk punch that remained in the crystal tumbler. He felt just fine.

XI · *Seduction*

They set out that afternoon, the three of them, for their picnic. The lieutenant, resplendent in his finest dress uniform, carried the woven raffia basket in which Frau Krasinska and Eugenie had carefully packed cold sausage, a terrine of duck, a loaf of bread, and two large bottles of white wine. It was a *fête champêtre*, a *déjeuner sur l'herbe*—which is to say, it had the quality of having been somehow posed. They weren't simply out there, walking in the meadows and woods and then stopping by the pond to have a meal but were conforming to a pattern as if there were some Platonic form of a picnic they were trying to embody. The women in their sundresses and matching parasols looked to have wandered out of a painting. This made the excursion easier for Stefan, who now had a more or less clear idea of how to comport himself.

Sonja, as she now insisted he call her (in acknowledgment of the morning's confession, or because of the informality of the occasion), was quietly observant, considering his plight and perhaps trying to decide whether she felt any disposition to grant him the favors for which he had announced himself a candidate. On the other hand, Eugenie was chatty. She limped along, not apparently in any pain but with an odd lurching gait by which she kept up well enough. It could have been her way of distracting attention from her physical disability, spinning webs of impressions, fantasies, little jokes, and literary allusions. She had been reading George Sand, of whom she fundamentally approved. And she had been marching through Manzoni and flirting with Fontane, who was a bit arch for her tastes. And of course there was Hugo . . .

"But do you read novels?" she asked. "Or do you prefer poetry as more aristocratic and therefore fitting for a hussar? Or is it the theater?"

"The theater," he said, although he had not been to many plays. He supposed that living off in this small town, Sonja and Eugenie would not have seen many plays either, but they both obviously read a great deal, devouring novels, poems, essays, short stories, and whatever else the postman could lug to them.

"One day," she said, "Mama and I shall go to Vienna or Paris and every night go to the theater to see another play. Great meals in fine restaurants, in *salons privés,* and then to the theater!"

"One does not need a *salon privé* when dining with one's mother," Sonja said.

"But we'll enter separately, and about each of us women people will wonder who is the lucky man to be having supper behind those drawn curtains and closed doors."

"Ridiculous," the mother said but not sharply. She was more wistful than dismissive. Stefan wanted very much to say something witty and comforting, to offer to take Eugenie, to offer to take them both, to turn their present destination, a spread blanket by the goose pond, into that *salon privé* of her dreams, but he could not come up with anything that wasn't either awkward or too forward, or even insulting to one or the other of his companions. "Perhaps we'll all go, one day, and . . . and celebrate something wonderful," he said. It was the best he could do.

"Your promotion, or your decoration for gallantry by the emperor!" Eugenie prompted. "And we'll commemorate that first picnic we had, so many years ago. This very picnic . . ."

"Yes, yes," he said, grateful and relieved. That was just what he had wanted, that exact quality.

It was not a long walk to the pond. Sonja no doubt had gauged the distance carefully, keeping her daughter's limitation in mind. As they spread the blanket Stefan was aware of a feeling of empathy. He realized what it must be like for this woman to have a bright, even gifted, and otherwise quite attractive daughter who was afflicted in this way. Poor daughter, and yet poor mother too, who must in some way blame herself for her child's deformity and must feel, therefore, a particular responsibility. That was, perhaps, why they lived here in the relative seclusion of Waldenburg. Quite possibly that lame foot was the reason for Sonja's never having remarried, or that and her feeling of obligation to her child. And yet, Sonja did not seem to labor under that obligation, but was solicitous, attentive, loving, and able to delight in the girl's brave gaiety.

Yes, yes, it was all as it should be, but he realized that there were interesting consequences to Sonja's generosity and self-sacrifice, consequences of particular relevance to himself. If she had not remarried for the girl's sake (or would not, until the girl herself married?), then she might, as a woman of some sensual experience, not to say abundant gift, find in his presence and abject need a degree of convenience, an opportunity that was not merely an occasion for her generosity and charity.

He was deluding himself. He was allowing the flimsiest wisps of association and random speculation to take on the look of solid construction. Still, he had to admit the question was real enough. Why hadn't she remarried? She would not have had any trouble attracting men. He could swear to that. And she was a good woman, comfortably fixed, with a poise and charm that were all the more impressive for her modesty and simplicity. She was, indeed, nothing less than wonderful . . .

He caught himself. He realized that he was falling in love, had already fallen, with a woman old enough to be his mother. With a woman whose daughter might be a more suitable match. And yet, the very absurdity of his love could also serve as its badge of honor. The quirky individuality of the human heart is not to be governed by the dreary expectations of a rigid society. Of course not, not for a free spirit like himself!

"Would you?" Eugenie was asking.

"I beg your pardon?" he said.

She smiled at him for his absentmindedness. "I asked if you would put the wine into the pond to cool."

"Certainly," he said. "Just into the water?"

There was a place farther down where the brook that ran from this little pond to the next and larger pond flowed through some shallows. There were small mossy stones against which the bottles could be propped so that the running water would cool the wine efficiently. "I'm afraid it's awkward for me," she said.

"Please, allow me," he replied, and he took the two large bottles down to that rocky place where the water ran fast and sibilant. We will drink wine, he thought, and the girl will fall asleep, tired from her having walked all this way from the house. Sonja and I will wander off into the woods to explore, and in a glade, soft with pine needles, we will sit down to rest and enjoy the wonderful pine smell, and we shall come together as slowly and easily as the sun and the sea come together at evening, with the leaning, and then the touching, and then at last the immersion of the one into the other.

Imagining it, he was becoming tumescent again. He began to jog in place, which was an old remedy he'd heard about back at school. There was another possible solution to his difficulty but he did not want to resort to that, not now. He realized that he was saving himself for her, which was a wonderful novelty that made him feel pure and noble, almost pious. For this grand self-denial, he believed himself destined to be rewarded. He had begun to deserve her love, had shown himself worthy. No doubt, this was what Goethe meant when he wrote that the eternal woman draws us upwards, Stefan thought, feeling a certain satisfaction at having thought of that phrase. Later on he would have to remember to refer to it. (Or should he wait until he had read the whole play?)

Back at the site of the picnic, where the geese had yielded

the near bank and were now paddling idly toward the opposite shore, the women were preparing the alfresco feast. Eugenie had made the terrine. She was learning how to do these more complicated dishes, she said, and would be grateful for the lieutenant's criticisms. He told her he knew little about fancy cooking, having eaten very simply at school and, before that, at his aunt and uncle's house.

"Your aunt and uncle's house?"

"My parents died when I was a boy," he explained.

"I'm sorry," Eugenie said.

"It was many years ago."

"Still," she said, "one has the feeling of loss. I miss my father."

"He died recently?"

"Three years ago," Sonja said. "A ruptured appendix."

"I'm sorry."

"These things happen," Sonja said. "Life goes on."

"The question," Eugenie announced, "is how it goes on. It may be that a death reminds us of our own impending death and is therefore a prompting to prayer and virtue. Or it could just as easily be a reminder to seize the day and get what pleasure we can from the brief time that remains to us in the sunlight. But unable to choose between the two, we do nothing and keep to our old habits, wasting our days from month to month and year to year. Is it not so?"

"Is what not so?" Stefan asked, uncertain which question she was posing, let alone what answer to make.

"Don't mind Eugenie. That's her way of playing. You'll get used to it," Sonja said. And to her daughter, she warned, "You'll frighten the lieutenant." But it was no real warning. She was obviously proud of her clever daughter, her flawed but all the more precious jewel.

"Is it not so," Eugenie repeated, "that a death prompts us to improve our lives, but we have no idea which way to go, how to improve them, or what we really want?"

"It may well be. I was too young, I think, to have any such thoughts. I was just stricken. I couldn't understand how there could be such a thing as death. I still can't, really."

"You mean an afterlife?" Eugenie asked.

"Well, yes. Do we have any sort of consciousness after we die? It is absurd to think so and impossible not to."

"Yes, yes! Exactly," Eugenie said. She made him feel very clever indeed. He was glad to have held up his end in the little duel of wits. He would not have liked to look stupid before Sonja. Or Eugenie either, for that matter.

"The wine must be chilled by now," Sonja suggested.

"I'll get it," he volunteered.

"One bottle, only. Leave the other in the water to stay cold."

"Good idea," he said.

He went to fetch the first bottle. They ate, drank, talked, and lay on the blanket, looking up at the slow motion of a cloud caressing the faded blue silk of the sky. He had it in mind that the wine and the sunshine might put Eugenie to sleep, so that he and Sonja could go off together for the second bottle, pause, embrace, and continue from there. But Eugenie chattered indefatigably. He got up and alone made the journey to fetch the second bottle. He poured the wine into their glasses, and resolved to try harder to be amusing and keep up his end of the conversation. The conventions of courtship, he realized, were confusing on this issue. In one way, the responsibility was the man's to charm and pursue, but then there was also the image of the strong, silent officer about whom the female chatter broke like jewels of sea spray at the sturdy prow of a ship. Stefan was grateful for that excuse for his silence, which could also cover a fair degree of awkwardness and stupidity. He coached himself not to try so hard. He told himself to relax and be patient, that there would be other afternoons, other occasions. Still, he found himself trying to will the girl into a drowsy doze and the mother into a restlessness that would only find ease in a walk somewhere. But of course it got mixed up somehow. The mother was the one who drifted off while the girl talked on about George Sand and Chopin and Musset, as if they were neighbors down the road.

In a way, it seemed quite funny, and Stefan was a good

enough sport to be able to laugh at his own misfortunes. He saw a kind of justice in his predicament, and as his punishment he forced himself to be attentive and lively in his conversation with Eugenie. Admittedly, this was not difficult, for she seemed able to go on without help for as long as she liked. Meanwhile, looking only occasionally at the mother, Stefan noticed the fullness of her lips now that she was asleep and how they quivered sometimes, either from her breathing or perhaps from a dream. It was not impossible that Eugenie might yet fall asleep. He could then wake Sonja with a kiss, or better yet kiss her so lightly, so delicately that she might incorporate the kiss into her dream, which he was by now convinced she must be having, although he dared not suppose himself to be its hero.

The afternoon had hung there, poised for a moment, but now it was moving on, the light changing, the wind coming up a bit from the east. Sonja awoke. The geese returned from their excursion across the pond to the place where they usually basked in the late afternoon sun and waited, somewhat annoyed, for the intruders to go away, which at last they did. Satisfied that he had not disgraced himself, Stefan was now nonetheless frustrated. He had expected some further progress, a sign, a look, but he had seen nothing at all to suggest any more reason for hope than there had been the day before. He was even sorry he'd let her know he wanted her. She was going to ignore it, evidently, and that was humiliating, what one might expect from a grown-up dealing with a presumptuous child. He considered another bottle of brandy but, remembering his hangover, decided that something less drastic would have to do. Rather than endure those physical tortures, he thought he'd prefer to lie there in his room, waiting for sleep's oblivion and release. Perhaps he might be able to form a better plan than just getting drunk.

He maneuvered through the evening—a light supper of omelettes and cheese and good fresh bread and then the entertainments. Eugenie played the spinet, performing pleasantly some of the preludes of her adored Chopin, and then they read aloud, the three of them taking turns from a leather-bound treasury of great poetry. At ten o'clock, Sonja at last announced it was time for her to be going to bed. Stefan said that he, too, would retire. Eugenie put away the music and the book. They all disappeared upstairs into their respective rooms.

He was sure that Sonja was amused by his abject declaration or, even worse than that, had forgotten it, having brushed it away as she might have done a gnat that had dared fly too close. He wasn't even worth thinking about.

What he should have done, of course, was to invite them both to come along when he went for the wine. The obviousness of that stratagem now all but overwhelmed him. Surely, Eugenie, with her bad foot, would have declined, and Sonja might have accepted. They would have had their opportunity. Sonja might even have been waiting for just such a signal on his part, but he'd never made it, had been too stupid even to think of it at the time. God, he was an oaf, a dunce, a buffoon! It was his own fault that he had made so little progress during the day. He had lost ground. She had been waiting, he was convinced, for some move from him, some gesture, however furtive and uncertain, of invitation . . .

He sighed. He got up, undressed, hung his uniform carefully on the hanger, got into bed, and blew out the candle on his nightstand. Outside, crickets chirped, or perhaps they were peepers. Stefan wasn't sure. But there was some boisterous celebration going on, an affirmation of either insect or amphibian life that the lieutenant had to endure along with its implied taunts. Those simple creatures could mate, teem, populate meadow and pond, and do it gracefully, singing all the while. He, meantime, lay alone, having outgrown his instinctual certainties but not yet having attained the conscious ability to plan and carry out what his most elementary instincts prompted.

He saw his way, now. He would tell his commander he had fallen hopelessly in love with the girl. He did not have to mention the girl's foot. All he needed to report was that she did not return his affection and that, therefore, he felt uncomfortable staying longer in the Krasinska house. The commander might smile at his youth and foolishness, but would certainly change his billet. Yes, yes, first thing Monday morning!

He felt better, relaxed now, and able to contemplate an eventual diminution of pain. He could even imagine sleep, which would make the hours fly by. He lay there, still hearing the crickets or frogs, or perhaps both, and the noises of the house, an occasional creak in a certain density of silence. But then he heard what sounded like footsteps, and felt as much as heard the opening of the door. He was dreaming, surely.

No, he was awake, and it was she, Sonja. She closed the door behind her and came to his bed. He could see now her finger at her lips in the sign for silence. She pulled down the counterpane, climbed into the bed beside him, and drew the cover back up.

He opened his mouth, about to speak. She put her finger to his lips. And then her lips to his lips.

"Shshsh."

XII · *Destiny*

Sometime during the night, when Stefan was asleep, she disappeared. He awoke, reached out, and found she was gone, but he had no doubt about the reality of what had happened, for he could not remember any dream being so vivid or continuous. In dreams, scenes change, people turn into other people, and while a woman may well come to visit in the night, she is more likely than not to beckon and then impose burdens and create improbable obstacles, so that one must spend the rest of the dream polishing boots or frantically looking for a misplaced belt buckle.

She had been there, but Stefan, reduced to his more primitive senses, had been unable to see much of her—or himself, for that matter. And while he had heard her breathing and its transformation into throaty sighs, he had not been able to exchange a single word with her. That was reasonable enough, he supposed. Clearly, she had not wanted Eugenie to be aware of what was going on just across the hallway. But with only touch, smell, and taste to rely on, Stefan found that his first experience of sexual intercourse had been less vivid, though more subtle, dreamlike, and abstract than he had expected.

He thought of going after Sonja, joining her in her bed as she had come to join him in his. But he wasn't sufficiently sure of himself. She had not invited him to follow her, and certainly he did not want to presume or risk losing her, now that he had her. The joy of his good fortune and the wonderful tingle he felt kept him entirely content for some minutes, but he soon began to think again, at least in a general way. He wondered, for instance, if he might expect other visits. Would this now become a regular pattern for the future? Would she come to visit every night? Or randomly, keeping to herself the added gift of surprise, bestowing her favors only as her own whims prompted?

He could even imagine a set of circumstances in which, for propriety's sake, and for Eugenie's too, there would be no daytime reference to the change in the relationship between him and Sonja. There would be an unspoken understanding that it was not to be referred to. But when Eugenie was not in the room? Or not at home? When only Sonja and Stefan were in the house together?

He would abide by whatever rules she set. He was happy and grateful, and . . . confident. It had been luck that had brought him here, sheer good fortune that had prompted the rearrangement of billeting assignments. It might just as easily have been Lieutenant Steinhardt or Lieutenant Czerny who was assigned to this paradise. But he, Stefan, had been the lucky one. He had to trust in that, and trust that his good luck would continue.

No, it had been more than luck. Luck is simply the cynic's way of describing destiny. It had been fated for the two of them to come together, decreed by the gods of love. Neither of them had known it, but each had been there in the other's future, waiting all those years and even aeons for exactly this conjunction.

If he believed that, as he saw no reason not to, then he could be confident about his prospects. In love and in war, luck would be loyal to him. He was a hussar, after all, and deserved no less.

He even saw a certain attractiveness in the situation, if it were to turn out as he had speculated. Sonja's requirement for absolute discretion was one he could live with easily enough for her sake, but for him it was a positive advantage. He recognized his inexperience and consequent unease in the role of lover. He might be saved that awkwardness, might reap all the benefits without having to exert himself to be courtly—gallant, witty, suave, and proficient in all those arts that only years of dalliance could teach. Instead, he could offer her his raw passion, dumb love, the true article that can be neither learned nor feigned.

Yes, it had been luck or even destiny, but he could see why she had come to him and even admire her for her ability to see through the nonsensical posturings of most men, seizing instead upon him for his deep, silent, and much more admirable love.

And he did love her.

He wondered what she looked like, naked.

XIII · *Advice*

Sunday morning Stefan had to ride to the garrison to attend the chaplain's services that were more or less obligatory for the officers, whom the commander expected to set a good example for the men. After church, there was the buffet, the most lavish meal of the week at the officers' mess. Stefan did not get back to the house until midafternoon. There was no occasion for him to approach Sonja privately until Eugenie went off to set the table for supper and supervise Wanda in the kitchen.

"I must speak with you," he said, not quite whispering.

"Why?"

He had no idea what to say. Wasn't it obvious? "Isn't it obvious?" he managed to ask.

"Not at all."

"But . . ."

She put her finger to her lips and smiled. Was that a promise? An offer? Or simply a reminder of her gift the previous night, a gift she could bestow or withhold as she pleased? A threat, then? Some subtle combination of all of these?

He had the impression that she was trifling with him and was at once delighted and discomforted. He had no clear sense of how to respond. What he would have liked to do was be self-assured and masterful and find some way of telling her bluntly to stop playing games. But he had no authority, could not command her to do anything, and was afraid that if he pushed too hard, he would lose even the hope of her returning one night to his bed.

In fact, she did not come that night. Stefan did not know what to think. During his grand buffet luncheon at the officers' mess on Sunday, he had felt he was a man among men, one who had his own private life, his secrets, his *affaires de coeur*. But now? He could not really think of what had happened as a conquest. She had consented, or had condescended, and he had been no more than her convenient plaything. In a way, he was worse off now than on Saturday afternoon, even more hopeless and impotent.

He was awake for hours, waiting for her to visit him again, wondering whether to go and visit her, and from time to time still considering the possibility of going to the commander to change his quarters. But that was no longer a real option. Now it would be an unequivocal defeat in which he'd be running away from her. She would be quite right to laugh at him for that.

He had to speak to her, had to clarify the rules of their situation. Sooner or later, he would find an opportunity. Given enough time and patience, he'd be able to address her and make his altogether justified complaint. Even if she were trying to avoid him, he'd contrive his moment. The house was not so large, nor the number of its occupants so great, that he could not confidently await that perfect opportunity.

It did not come on Monday or Tuesday either, but on Wednesday afternoon, when he returned somewhat earlier than usual, Wanda was out in the herb garden and Eugenie not yet back from a visit to a neighborhood friend. Sonja was alone in the living room.

"You do not come to my room any more?" he said, going right to the point. Or to one of the points uppermost in his mind.

"I haven't, no."

"Why not?" he asked.

"I haven't felt like it."

"What have I done?"

"Nothing," she told him. "It has to do more with my own mood."

"That's not fair."

"What has fairness to do with these things?"

"I don't understand why you came to me in the first place," he said.

"No, probably not. But you had been mooning after me so prettily all afternoon," she said. "It pleased me."

"And never again?"

"I don't promise either way. It could happen tonight, or in a month. Or not for a year."

"But that's terrible," he protested.

"It's honest."

"Don't you care for me at all?"

"I hadn't thought about it," she said, "but perhaps I do, a little. You're a sweet boy."

It was not what he wanted to hear, but he could not argue and throw away his one small advantage. Instead, he could try in one *coup de main* to take the high ground. "But I love you," he declared.

"You hardly know me," she said.

"Knowing and loving are not the same thing," he insisted.

"Loving and sex are not the same, either."

"I think about you all the time," he said. That was true enough, even if some of his thoughts were less than adoring.

"That's very dear."

"Will you come to me again?" he asked, not quite pleading but close to it.

"I might," she said, "perhaps." And then, after a coquettish pause, "Probably."

He burned. She found him amusing? Then he would amuse her. "Now?"

"Don't be silly."

"But why not?"

"There are no whys. It has to do only with my inclinations. But if that won't do, I don't like to rush. And it is almost suppertime. Eugenie will be home soon. It's not how I like these things to be arranged."

"We must go away, spend a weekend together."

"I'll think about it. But don't be greedy. I may come to you some night when you least expect it. Perhaps even because you least expect it."

"I don't understand!"

"You will, one day. And you'll think of me."

He thought she was teasing him. And yet he was sure she would come that night, tiptoe into his room, pull down the coverlet once more, and join him again, touching, nibbling, and finally writhing in exquisite intricacy. And when she did not, he assumed it was because he had been expecting her. He hardly slept. He lay there while his hope gave way to dejection, which turned to rage, which softened to remorse, which in turn froze to a sardonic amusement at his ridiculous predicament.

The next day, at the garrison, he confided in Fritzl, his batman, in whose simple earthiness he hoped to find some new idea of how to proceed. It wasn't what he wanted to do, but he was desperate, unable himself to think of any way of taking the initiative back into his own hands. (Back? Had he ever had it?) "Oh, terrible, terrible. I've no idea what to do."

"And what seems to be the lieutenant's problem?" Fritzl asked, delighted to have his master's confidence.

"It's a matter of some delicacy," Stefan began.

"A touch of the clap, sir?"

"Hardly," Stefan said.

"The pox, then?"

"No."

"Why, then, the master must be in love," Fritzl said, his moon-faced grin blooming forth.

"I can rely on you not to carry tales?"

"No, sir," Fritzl said. "You'd be a fool to believe me just because I promised you I'd keep still. But you can rely on yourself. You have the power to break me from corporal back to private, to make my life miserable. You know that and I know it. What you can trust is that I depend on you."

"Yes, I see," Stefan said. "Actually, it was that kind of . . . How shall I say? Directness?"

"Realism, sir?"

"Exactly. Realism. It was that kind of realism I hoped you might be able to supply."

"I'll do my best, sir."

"Or worst," Stefan said, encouraged by his ability still to make jokes. In brief outline, he described the situation at the Krasinska household. Fritzl managed to contain his reaction, betraying neither amusement or disapproval. Stefan might have been presenting a problem in differential calculus.

Fritzl was the perfect listener, polishing a brass buckle so that he did not have to look his master in the eye and yet signifying by the slow rhythm of his work that his mind was altogether on the words the lieutenant was speaking. It had the same pretension to anonymity that a confessional has, even though that is only a pretension and both parties know perfectly well who is on the other side of the grille. From time to time, Fritzl asked a clarifying question. Finally, when the lieutenant had finished his poignant but nearly useless descriptions of his doubts, torments, and discomforts, Fritzl asked him, "But what is it you want? You must decide that, first of all."

"I want her to come again. I want her to visit often. I want her to come when *I* please."

"Ah, yes. Well, then, you seem to be going about it the wrong way. You are making yourself abject. You want to do the opposite, you know."

"But how?" Stefan wanted to know.

"You must make her jealous."

Stefan laughed. It was an absurd idea.

"Why is the lieutenant laughing?" Fritzl asked, looking at him now.

"But you can't be serious. How can I make her jealous? She doesn't care for me."

"She cared enough to come to bed with you. She cares. All women care. They care more than we do, believe me."

"I still don't understand . . ."

64

"If the lieutenant will permit a suggestion?"

With a gesture of upturned palms that signified either utter befuddlement or the willingness to receive whatever Fritzl had to offer, the lieutenant waited, more patient than expecting anything useful.

"Court the daughter," Fritzl said.

Slowly, the lieutenant lowered his hands to his sides. He thought about it a moment, then another few moments, and then gradually began to understand it was conceivable. More than simply conceivable, it was plausible. It was . . .

"Brilliant," he said. "Fritzl, you're brilliant."

"The lieutenant does me too much honor."

XIV · *Review*

And had he come, instead, to me? Would I have been able to advise him differently or better?

Those are two quite separate questions, of course. It is unlikely that a young man in Stefan's position, feeling unsure of himself and perplexed, would have compounded his risk by baring his breast to a superior officer. The traditions of regimental camaraderie notwithstanding, I was a captain and he was a newly commissioned second lieutenant. There was a chasm between us that personal charm was unlikely to bridge. Still, it was theoretically possible, and I have sometimes regretted not having sent out that signal of friendship, of availability, or of mere human fellow-feeling that could have given him the necessary spark of confidence.

But even so, what would I have suggested to him that would have been much different from the advice of that miserable batman? In a purely practical way, Fritzl was shrewd enough. It would have required a different attitude toward life, a generosity, a *profondeur* Fritzl lacked, and even a world-weariness no longer greedy for possessions and experiences to counsel young Stefan to accept as a gift those visits that were obviously meant as a gift. To enjoy the suspense. To accede to the situation and his inability to control its progress. Life is like that, after all. Illusion, the desire for more, the pictures in our minds . . . these are not worth letting go of the treasures within our grasp, are they?

Well, perhaps I might have said some such words. But would I have been eloquent enough to persuade him? Could anyone have managed to force him to see what his youth and zest and lust could not immediately comprehend? I regret, but I cannot blame myself.

In the odd moments available to him for reflection during the course of his duties, Stefan found increasing merit and a wonderful justice in Fritzl's suggestion. If Sonja were telling the truth about her lack of emotional commitment and if she honestly did not love him, then she would not be likely to feel jealousy and would not react to his stratagem. She would be invulnerable to the feint he was now considering. On the other hand, if she had been lying to him—or to herself, which was always possible, even in a woman of a certain age and with some degree of experience—then she would in one way or another betray herself. He would have her where he wanted her, and whenever he wanted her. She would be afraid of losing him.

Stefan had a good many opportunities for this kind of consideration and contemplation. The military life requires the attendance of the body but often gives in return moments or even hours of mental leave. To stand stiffly at attention on parade becomes a matter of habit and reflex. The intelligent soldier learns to let his mental faculties stand at ease, even to dismiss them entirely for a certain period, keeping only a skeleton crew on duty. He must know which is his left foot. He must keep his chin in and his shoulders back. He must remember how to count by fours. For the rest of his brain, however, there are the joys of mathematical puzzles and word games, silent rehearsals of operas and operettas, or the pleasures of fantasy, sentimental, adventurous, or pornographic as the taste of the soldier and the mood of the moment dictate. Stefan had what he realized was fundamentally a military problem to solve. It was, as Fritzl had described it, a question of strategy and tactics. It is no accident, he decided, that men talk of their conquests in the boudoir using the same words as they employ for triumphs on the battlefield. As often as not, the same kind of thinking has produced the success.

Stefan saw, for example, that if his feint was going to be successful, it would have to be convincing. He could not expect to impress Sonja with any perfunctory display of attention to Eugenie. It would have to be a serious commitment of his forces. This feigning would not be difficult. Indeed, as Stefan stood out there on the parade ground with his ceremonial sword held upright before him, he recalled that vision of Eugenie's shadow against the bathroom curtain. He would be able to address himself to her with an authentic zeal. In fact, now that he thought about it, he began to wonder if there might not have been some flirtatiousness on Eugenie's part in all that talk about George Sand and Chopin and Musset. She approved of Sand, admired her. As a novelist? Or as a woman who wore trousers, smoked cigars, and took lovers, perhaps in *salons privés* of fashionable restaurants?

How had he failed to notice that the girl was coming as close as she could to issuing an invitation. Or a challenge. Well, it was not too late for him to respond. And if he succeeded?

That was not an issue he was quite prepared to face. The mother was less intimidating because she was older and was unsuitable as a possible wife. It did not even have to be said, because it was obvious to both parties, that the marriage of an officer of hussars in his early twenties and a widow in her forties was altogether out of the question. The result was a kind of candor that informed their intercourse. Dalliance was simply dalliance, and the possibilities for misunderstandings were limited (although they were, heaven knew, grave enough). With the daughter, though, he'd be venturing on more treacherous ground. She was excluded neither by her age nor by her social class from thinking about a marriage to an officer in a fashionable regiment. On the other hand, Stefan could imagine her limping up the aisle of a church and lurching along under the crossed swords of his fellow officers, whose training and discipline would just barely suppress their condescending smiles.

He felt terrible for her and also for himself. He could not subject her to that cruel laughter. He would not subject himself to it. The poor thing. And yet, he realized that part of his distress was from the idea of being laughed at, himself. He could understand how he would react if one of his brother officers were to enter into such a marriage, and that understanding pained him as an act of treachery to Eugenie.

No, no. He could not marry her. And as long as he kept that clearly in mind, there would be a limit to his commitment to her, a counterweight that would keep him from any irresponsible behavior. Every step, each moment would have to be calculated. It would be a point of honor not to treat her badly.

Still, there was room for speculation. If George Sand was the girl's heroine, did that not perhaps suggest that she might be aware, herself, of her limited matrimonial prospects? Or, at the least, that she was ready for a little naughty fun, if only the opportunity could be contrived? It was only a lame step or two from that thought to the fantasy of an arrangement in which he might visit one or the other bedroom, might have one Krasinska or the other come to visit him, might even have the delightful task of having to distinguish by feel, scent, and taste which of them was in bed with him.

"Company, left . . . face!"

When the captain's command rang out, Stefan turned as smartly as any of the other lieutenants in front of their platoons. The regimental flags and battalion pennants fluttered in the breeze. The body awaited the next command.

"Forward march!"

And it marched.

XV · *The Feint*

Inasmuch as Sonja was making every effort to keep clear of Stefan, either in order to tease him or to keep him from boring her with his importunity, he found himself several times that week in Eugenie's company. This was just the opportunity he wanted. On Tuesday evening, for example, he returned to the house from a long day of inspection of sanitary facilities in various neighborhood outposts to find Eugenie sitting with her book in the living room.

"Mama has gone to bed," the young woman announced. "She has a touch of the vapors."

"That's a shame," Stefan said, delighted. "Would it disturb you if I joined you? Or would you prefer to read alone?"

"Please, join me. I'd be happy to have company," she said, patting the sofa cushion beside her.

It was a warm invitation. He had been blind not to have noticed such signals before this. He wondered, as he sat down, whether the great joke might not be that the girl had fallen in love with him and been pining after him all the time he had been yearning for her mother. "Still reading, I see," he said, nodding at her book.

"It's what I mostly do."

"I suppose it improves the mind," he said, affably enough.

"In some ways," she concurred, "but it can also be misleading. It does not happen in the world, although it invariably does in novels, that the good people come to good ends, 'living happily ever after,' while wicked characters come to bad ends. The danger is that one may try to live in the world as if it were a novel. Don't you agree?"

70

"Oh, yes," he said, "quite," thinking that he had to forge boldly ahead. "Particularly with regard to relations between the sexes."

"Exactly," she said. "One might almost imagine that there was a conspiracy of novelists to frighten foolish virgins."

"And you are not frightened?" he asked.

"No."

"Or foolish?"

"I hope not."

He looked at her and was struck by her frank smile as she disclosed her awareness of his appraisal. She was a delicate creature with slender wrists and a long neck that suggested poignant fragility. She had silky hair of a peculiarly metallic color, brightly burnished to a tone between brown and blond, and pale, clear skin. She spent much of her life indoors, where her lame foot did not impede her as it would have out in the woods and fields. She had, then, a certain air of refinement, a hothouse quality.

Her bosom, he noticed, was higher and smaller than her mother's, and her hips flared only slightly. He had observed on the way to the goose pond how she looked almost boyish sometimes from the back. But it was her eyes, and the way she looked at him, basking in his attention, reveling in it, all but defying him to make the next move, that made the greatest impression upon him.

"Or any of those things?"

"Nobody is perfect," she said.

He understood that she was being ambiguous about the question of her virginity, but there was no possible ambiguity about her attitude toward him.

"We're all human," he said, excusing her, if that was indeed what she had implied.

"I had begun to wonder about you," she said. "You were such a proper and correct young officer when we went on our picnic, paying attention to Mama and pretending to ignore me . . ."

"But you saw through that," he said. He couldn't believe his luck.

"I wasn't sure."

It was as close to a command as he was likely to get. He took her in his arms and kissed her. She responded ardently. He was delighted but remembered his promises to himself about honorable conduct. He had to let her know that this was no more than a diversion, an amusement. He was not a serious suitor, but it would not be his fault if, having declared himself to be a vile seducer, he found only a warmer welcome for his candor or conformity to the standards of romantic villainy in fiction.

Her hands were roaming the back of his neck like small grazing animals. Her hungry kisses left him gasping for air. He broke free to ask, "Where is Wanda?"

"In her room, asleep, I suppose."

"And your mother?"

"As I said, she's upstairs."

"But not asleep. We could be interrupted."

"It's unlikely."

"But possible," he said.

"Are you afraid? I'm not!"

"I'm afraid for you, then," he said. "It would be safer and more comfortable, too, if I were to come to you later on, don't you think?"

"I suppose."

"But you know that this is a reckless thing to be doing. I'm not rich. I can't afford to get married. I shall be taking advantage of you."

"Or, the other way around. I could be taking advantage of you. That's possible, too, isn't it?" she asked.

"Like George Sand?"

"Exactly."

"No ties? No commitments? No promises?"

"None," she said. Her intention was to be magnificent, and he was willing to concede her accomplishment.

"You're an admirable woman," he said, "but it's a dangerous way to live."

"Life is danger. The alternative is not to live at all," she said. "Only those things we are willing to throw away are what we can be said truly to possess. The rest possesses us."

He wasn't altogether sure he understood what she meant. She had read it in a book somewhere, no doubt. But in a practical way, its meaning was clear enough—that she would welcome him as a visitor.

He couldn't think sufficiently quickly, couldn't decide whether this was better or worse than what he had intended. His fantasy from the parade ground returned, in which he enjoyed both of them as his whim of the moment dictated, the quiet, luxurious embraces of the mother or the more strenuous and lively ardors of the daughter. As a practical matter, and for the prevention of awkward encounters in the upstairs hallway, he realized that he ought always to be the visitor. Otherwise, they'd bump into each other in his room.

Both of them together? He put that thought aside, or struggled free of it.

"You don't believe in love?" he asked her.

"I believe in loving. The other tends to turn into possessiveness and domesticity. Women have been enslaved for centuries now by what they have been told was love. Loving, on the other hand, never enslaves. Giving and sharing do not enslave."

"Wonderful!" he said, relieved to have all burden of dishonor lifted from his conscience. "And I must say, I feel . . . very loving toward you at this moment."

"And I toward you," she said.

Again, they embraced. He had the peculiar notion that their real selves were across the room somewhere, perched perhaps above the étagère, looking down approvingly at the two conjoined bodies on the sofa below. Meanwhile, his lips, his chest, his fingertips explored and delighted in her softness, leanness, fullness, and sweetness.

"I knew," she whispered, "from the first moment I set eyes on you, that this would happen."

"I didn't know, but I hoped," he said, remembering how his hopes had been conceived even before he'd set eyes on her. But it would not be flattering to let her know that.

"You'll come to me tonight," she said.

"Oh, yes."

"You'll be quiet."

"Of course," he said, thinking how wonderful it was. They were both creatures of darkness and silence.

"When?"

"When it's safe," he said.

They went around putting out lamps and checking the locks on the windows. She led the way upstairs. He followed, carrying the candlestick. At the top of the stairs, he waited for her to get the candlestick from her room and take a light from his. They kissed once more, and then she went into her room and closed the door behind her.

In his own room, as he undressed and put on his nightshirt, he thought how the prospect of an assured welcome was as delicious as the anticipation of a new sexual partner. Outside of bordellos, he supposed that the combination of these quite distinct delights was unusual, even for captains and majors with vastly more experience than he could claim. But if the immediate future was perfectly agreeable, the prospect of the coming days and weeks was puzzling. How long would he be able to keep this new liaison a secret? What would be the result of Sonja's discovery of his affair with Eugenie? He had intended her to find out about it, but he had not been able to foresee such instant and complete success. He wasn't even sure now what he wanted. What if he found he preferred Eugenie? Her talk was delightfully amusing. She had, somehow, the ability to make him feel more clever in her company than he ever was with anyone else. She was original and obviously ardent.

He got into bed and extinguished the candle. He would wait an hour. Or at least half an hour. Then he'd make a trip to the bathroom and, if there was no light shining through the crack below Sonja's door, he'd know it was safe to venture across the hallway to Eugenie's room. If the light in Sonja's room was still burning, he'd get a drink of water and return to his own room without having compromised himself or Eugenie.

But sooner or later, the chances were that there'd be some stupid slipup. One of them would find out about the other, and the moment that happened, they'd unite against him, loyal to each other. He'd be out, back in the barracks or assigned to another billet. But it would be an honorable withdrawal. He would be officially reprimanded, but privately praised. He could already imagine the winks of admiration. So the worst that could happen was acceptable and better than he could have hoped for only a few days ago.

He gave himself over to a less cerebral reverie, trying to project from what he already knew of Eugenie's body to what he would soon learn about the rest of it. How strange that a girl so innocent could be, at the same time, so lubricious. It occurred to Stefan that lubricity was a very clinical and specific description. He thought of her, across the hallway, beyond the door, in her bed, waiting for him, lubricious, lubricated . . . He could feel himself aroused.

The door opened.

The fool! She'd ruin everything. Her mother would hear them. This wasn't what they'd agreed. Why couldn't women take orders and carry them out?

"What are you . . . ?" he began to ask, but he felt a finger on his lips, silencing him. Just like her mother, he thought. And then he realized it was her mother.

"I didn't expect you," he whispered.

"I know," she said. "That's why I came. One doesn't like to be taken for granted."

She slipped into bed beside him and was flattered to find him ready for her, as if he had been lying there all those nights waiting, impatiently tumescent.

"How sweet!" she whispered. He felt the tip of her tongue in his ear and her fingertips wandering lightly elsewhere. But the most exquisite and perverse part of it was imagining Eugenie, across the hallway, waiting for him and imagining this, and this, and this. Could he contrive a way of managing to visit her later on? Would he have the stamina? What possible excuse could he invent if he failed to show up? She would be furious now, would despise him. Sonja would learn of his intended infidelity and she, too, would despise him. It would all be ruined, ruined.

But there are kinds of ruin too wonderful not to be enjoyed. He gave himself over at last to his destruction as she mercilessly laid him waste.

XVI · *The Impostors*

In the morning, Stefan woke early, dressed, and rode away, perhaps exercising more than ordinary care about not making unnecessary noise. He assumed that Eugenie would be furious. But what could he tell her? Could he claim to have fallen asleep? Could one do such a thing? He began to imagine a sequence of events in which he would have waited longer and longer, in order to ensure their safety and privacy, until he had waited too long and just drifted off. He could swear to have done so, express his regrets, and declare his passion.

He did not for a moment expect to be believed. He had lost her. If only he had gone to her earlier . . . Of course, in that case, Sonja would have discovered an empty bed, would have gone to look for him, would no doubt have found him in bed with Eugenie. Had he been lucky, then, having narrowly escaped? He hardly knew what to think.

At the garrison, when Fritzl inquired about his progress, Stefan reported his confusion. Fritzl listened respectfully, endured patiently all manner of irrelevant information about how lively and charming Eugenie was and what her views were, and picked out nuggets of useful fact wherever he could find them. At last, when the lieutenant yielded the floor, the batman inquired, "But what does the lieutenant want? You have to decide that yourself, you know. No one can advise you which woman to prefer. It's only when you know where you want to go that you can chart how to get there."

"True enough," Stefan conceded.

"And so? Which woman is it? Whom do you want?"

"I want them both," the lieutenant blurted out, ashamed of himself.

"That won't be easy."

"No," Stefan admitted.

"Sooner or later, you will be compromised. It's inevitable," Fritzl warned.

"I know."

"Why not accept the one you've got? She's safer. She expects less of you. It's an arrangement most men would envy."

"Yes," the lieutenant agreed. "But it may be already too late for that. The way things have gone with the daughter, I may not be able to extricate myself so easily."

"We try to ensure against failure," Fritzl said, and then, flashing an impudent smile, "but what surprises us is success. Who could have figured on such a thing?"

"I'm not blaming you," Stefan reassured him.

"What you might do, if everything else fails," the corporal suggested, "is to tell the truth."

"Tell whom?"

"The girl. Tell her that you and her mother are . . . involved. And that you were trying to make the mother . . ."

"Jealous?"

"More attentive. Less sure of herself. She will go to her mother, who will perhaps be flattered. Or she will not. In either case, you will have preserved your relationship with the widow. The daughter's anger will eventually subside. It seems the least dangerous course."

"I'll consider it," Stefan said.

"Only as a last resort, mind you. And only if you decide you can content yourself with the mother. As I say, that's a choice you must make on your own, without advice."

Stefan drew on the boots that Fritzl had polished and stood patiently as the corporal brushed his tunic, adjusted his elegant shako, and rearranged a loop of braid at one shoulder. "Very good, sir," the batman pronounced, and stood aside for Stefan to inspect himself in the cheval glass.

"Yes, it will do," the lieutenant agreed, and he strode out to the parade ground.

He was possessed, however, by a feeling of hollowness, as though the uniform were real enough but somehow empty. He knew what Fritzl had told him was right and even obvious. But he could not imagine himself hurting the girl, as he knew he would now have to do. As he had already hurt her.

It was a terrible discovery to make—that he had no stomach for the casualties that were probably inevitable in the lists of love. The line from the song about how "we play our parts / At making love and breaking hearts" seemed heartless indeed. He had realized how love and war were both ruinous in their disregard of the niceties of civil behavior, but he had not quite brought himself to the point of imagining a poor afflicted girl like Eugenie and how she could be robbed of her self-regard, her spirit, not to say her honor. It was bad enough that young men like him had to die in battles in the meaningless conflicts between red tunics and blue, or round helmets and ridged ones. But that was the risk the men and officers had understood and accepted. He felt sorry for the horses who seemed innocent, having agreed to no such gamble.

The effect of these speculations and, even more important, of the feeling that prompted them was a growing conviction that he was a fraud, a mere poseur who had no business marching around in the resplendent uniform of a regiment of tough-minded men of the world who were ready for love and death, willing to accept the hard bargains that life offered, eager for honor and triumph, and careless of the cost. He was small-souled, a clerk at heart, a fellow of finical delicacy, an impostor.

He drilled himself through his day's duties, however, and after a light supper in the officers' mess rode homeward having resigned himself to the inevitable confrontation with Eugenie. His first attempt would be to claim that he had fallen asleep. If that worked, he'd try to retreat gracefully and see what he could do to save her feelings and his own. But if she did not believe him—as he was sure she would not—then he would tell her the truth as Fritzl had counseled him to do. He would lose her, of course. But he would regain some sense of honest dealing.

He put his horse in the barn, set out its oats, and walked slowly to the front door of the house, as if he were taking himself into some court-martial where he expected the outcome to be one of those humiliating ceremonies in which an officer rips off his epaulets and cuts away his tunic buttons with the point of a sharpened bayonet.

"Ah, lieutenant," Eugenie called out cheerily from the living room, "we've been waiting for you. You'll take a cup of tea with us, I hope?"

"Yes, please do, lieutenant," Sonja echoed. Her intonation was not so theatrically cheerful.

"I've been telling Mama all about us," Eugenie said, before he could frame a graceful way to decline.

"All?" he asked.

"How we became lovers last night," Eugenie said.

"I see," Stefan said. He was lying, of course, and saw nothing at all. He had no idea why she was saying this. He also knew that Sonja could not possibly believe her. Sonja had been with him most of the night. On the other hand, one did not like to contradict a young lady, particularly Eugenie. It all depended, he supposed, on what she meant by the word *lovers*. In a certain sense, they had indicated an intention to each other. Unable to decide what to say, he said nothing, which was tantamount to an admission. He stood there in the doorway of the large room, waiting to be reproached.

"You will have tea? Or would you prefer a coffee?" Sonja asked.

"Tea, if you'd be so kind."

"By all means," she said.

He came into the room and took one of the spindly chairs that flanked the sofa.

"I was surprised by Eugenie's news," Sonja said, handing him a delicate teacup and saucer.

"I can imagine," Stefan said. He did not smile, kept any hint of feeling from his voice. He might have been discussing the weather.

"I had no idea you were interested in her," Sonja said. "But, of course, as her mother, I'm delighted for you both, as long as you make each other happy. My only concern is that she not be hurt."

"Of course," Stefan said.

"As a man of honor, that would be your concern and responsibility as well, would it not?" the mother asked.

Stefan agreed. "Oh, quite. Yes, indeed." Was there a chance that Sonja might even approve? But of what would she approve? Had he become a suitor for Eugenie's hand, a candidate for marriage? This was not what he had expected.

He could see it, however, as Eugenie's elegant gesture of revenge.

She could say whatever she liked. The mother would back her up. And the two of them together would defy him to prove them wrong. As carefully as he held his teacup, so did he hold his fury at the way in which these women, by lying, could make him out to be a villain. This cunning woman and her crazy daughter? Their word against that of an officer and a gentleman? It was outrageous and absurd that they should be instantly believed.

"Of course, I haven't yet told Eugenie about *us*," Sonja continued, in a conversational, almost playful way, "about how you and I have been lovers. Do you think the news will upset her?"

"I should hope not," he replied evenly. "Are you upset, Eugenie, by your mother's disclosure?"

"Not in the least," Eugenie answered.

"I'm delighted to hear you say so," Stefan said. He sipped his tea, put the cup down carefully, and stood. He clicked his heels together in the Prussian fashion and bade them both a very good evening.

The temptation, as he closed the door of his room, was to collapse on his bed in helpless laughter. It had had the brittle air of a theatrical scene, and he'd got through it, which was a wonderful and exhilarating feeling. He hadn't understood either one of them, had barely known what to say, himself, but by going along with whatever they said, he'd kept matters from turning into the debacle that seemed at every instant to impend. Only later, on his way upstairs, had he realized that Sonja did not believe her daughter. And that Eugenie did not believe her mother. They were each now saying these things to the other in order to have established, later on, when the truth transpired, what a perfect confession had been made, how nothing secretive or furtive had been contemplated, and that each had been candid with the other all along.

XVII · *Words Made Flesh*

Lying in bed once more, he fancied himself to be some kind
of invalid who had only to allow time to glide by in order
to observe what fevers, sweats, chills, agonies, intervals of
euphoria, and occasional periods of respite in dreamless
sleep its passage could produce. He snuffed out the candle
and in the darkness listened to the chatter downstairs. Were
they talking about the revelations and claims they had exchanged? Or were they ostentatiously avoiding reference to
their defiant vaunts of so short a time ago?

They were not mad, but they weren't like ordinary people
either. They had, he supposed, strange notions of how
people in the fashionable quarters of cosmopolitan cities
lived and thought and spoke, and apparently they were trying
to abide by those outré rules. It was glamorous, sophisti-
cated, and, finally, stupid. But it was more than convenient
for Stefan's fantasy of enjoying the embraces of both women.
Ordinarily an utterly hopeless ambition, it seemed not so
unrealistic after all. Fritzl would be surprised. The limitations of cynicism, Stefan thought, lay precisely in its failure
to see the possibility of great good fortune or to seize opportunities for it that arose from time to time in otherwise normal lives.

He heard footsteps on the stairs and waited for mother and
daughter to separate to their own rooms. Would Sonja come
to him again? He thought not. Would Eugenie visit him or
expect his visit? He doubted it. He waited only a little while
after the light was extinguished in the hall, and then, quietly

if not quite furtively, crossed the six feet or so that separated his room from Eugenie's. He tried her door. It was not locked. He opened it, entered, closed it behind him, and hesitated until he could make out, by the starlight that filtered in through the windows, where the girl's bed was.

"Stefan?" she whispered, helping him find her.

"Yes."

"Over here," she said. It was at the same time an instruction and an invitation.

He found the bed, sat down on the mattress edge, and asked her, "What was that all about? Are you crazy? Are both of you crazy?"

"Aren't you glad?"

"I don't know. It's difficult to keep up with you both."

"Is that a double-entendre?"

"I hadn't intended it," he admitted.

"You're honest to say so, but honesty won't get you far in this household."

"Won't it?"

"Are we going to spend the whole night in elegant *causerie*, or are you going to get into bed with me?"

He got into bed.

"Do you like dirty talk?" she asked.

He put his finger to her lips. It was a trick he'd recently learned. She stopped chattering.

He was not really surprised to discover—too late to put the knowledge to any use, to retrieve the situation, or retreat gracefully from the commitment he had made—that she was, for all her bold, bright, witty, and provocative talk, a virgin.

And had he not known? Had he not mockingly put the question and been mockingly put off? Would he not, out of decency and kindness, at least have hesitated, giving her time to think further about whether she was sure she wanted him to come to her this way? When he asked himself these questions later that night, back in his own bed in his own room, he was candid enough to admit that he couldn't say, that he just didn't know. He admired Eugenie, mad though she was. At least she had the seriousness to act upon her beliefs, however peculiar they might be. He thought she was quite a young woman. He remembered the stock question girls were supposed to ask all the time, although no one had ever asked it of him: "Will you respect me, afterward?"

He respected her. He wasn't so sure what he thought about himself.

XVIII · *An Understanding*

When he awoke the next morning, Stefan was surprised to see that a note had been left for him on his nightstand. He reached over, picked it up, and read it. "It is essential that we have a private conversation at the earliest possible moment. S. Krasinska."

He stared at it. How very formal! He supposed that challenges to duels, warrants for executions, and other such dire messages partook of this same laconic style, having no need for rhetorical embellishment. The simple truth could be powerful enough. He could not help noticing that she had given her last name—her husband's name, really—and withheld her own, except for the grudging initial. He could imagine her jealousy and rage. Had she come sneaking in while he slept? Or, before that, had she observed, from the door to her room deliberately left ajar, his comings and goings during the night, confirming the unlikely but undeniable truth of her daughter's extravagant claim? He felt chagrin at having caused her pain. He had been a fool, had allowed himself to let fantasy get in the way of his perception of what ordinary people could stand, how they would necessarily react, and finally the nature of his own actions. He had ignored both women and had become a monster, himself. Now, they would ruin each other and him too. Or more likely they would turn upon him, uniting in their jealousy and contempt to reaffirm their ties of blood and do him whatever injury they could contrive together.

What fury she must have felt! "S. Krasinska" indeed. But why had she left the note for him when she might just as easily have wakened him, ordering him on the instant out of her house? Wouldn't that have been more satisfying? He tried to picture her writing the note, coming into his bedroom, putting it down on the nightstand . . . Of course! At that moment, the room had been empty, the bed deserted. She had come in with the note, knowing he was not there, and had left it for him to discover either upon returning from his foray across the hall or now, upon awaking.

He felt a temptation to flee. He could even hear in his ear the pounding of a pulse as his heart pumped away to supply his muscles the energy they would need if he were to make a dash for it, this very moment, into the darkness of the woods and far away to safety. But his mind understood that there was no safety. Flight would only compound his difficulties, adding desertion to the list of his other crimes and misdemeanors. His legs, frustrated of their impulse, felt leaden. It was all he could do to draw on the cumbersome elegance of those high boots. Would Sonja be waiting for him downstairs, her baleful eyes fixed upon the landing where his feet would first appear? Were both of them sitting together, expecting him to descend? He dreaded the meeting, but he also dreaded the way it would color the day, darkening it and stretching it out. To get the interview over now, face the worst and endure its torments was in some ways better than letting it loom crazily, grow, and writhe in his imagination. The day would be a wallow of self-accusation and abasement.

Sonja was no fool. She had known enough about these things to understand how he would be his own torturer. She had even seen that the spark of decency left in him would smolder away, as hot as her own anger.

He let his horse have its head and allowed himself to be carried along the familiar route, taking note that the sun was shining, that the air was crisp and fresh, and that it was the kind of day in which, ordinarily, a young, healthy man like

himself would exult, happy to be alive. Instead, he felt op-
pressed by how far he had fallen from that simple joy. Indeed, he supposed he ought to be feeling at least a shadow of
the triumph he had won, having wrested from the grudging
world if only for a moment the fulfillment of his fantasies.
But his victory had been so fleeting. He'd gone back to bed,
chastened by his discovery of Eugenie's innocence. He'd
fallen asleep. And then he'd awakened to the unqualified in-
dictment by the mother, whom he had, in every way, betrayed.

   He deserved every possible humiliation. Death, itself,
which would provide a kind of amnesty, was far too good for
him. Perhaps he could contrive some border incident, some
petty skirmish in which he might be killed . . . But, no, it
was too farfetched a thing even to dream of. The border was,
for one thing, absolutely quiet. For another, he was not
scheduled to be posted out there for a month yet. Finally,
even if the right conditions were to present themselves,
Stefan did not have any great confidence in his luck. He
would not be killed. Only his soldiers. And one or two on the
other side, all innocent men. The result would be an even
greater dishonor than the one he'd already brought upon
himself. He would be drummed out of the regiment. How
could he have allowed such things to happen? How could he
have been so stupid?

   All day long, there were references to love. Stefan might
have suspected a cosmic practical joke in which the entire
regiment conspired to rub his nose in his misfortune. His batman, his fellow officers, his men, who went about their duties
humming sentimental songs, even the colonel's nieces, who
had come to visit Waldenburg, dressed in frilly frocks with
matching parasols, one in lilac and the other in daffodil
yellow, all seemed to have appeared from a scene in some
light opera. Stefan was not introduced to the young ladies—
one was perhaps sixteen and the other fourteen—and for this
he was grateful. He thought of the perils that awaited them
in life, the designs of wicked men like himself. How long

was it since Eugenie had been just like one of these young girls?

I remember that lunch, of course, because the colonel's nieces had visited in the morning. The subject for discussion was love and its consequences—a new Symposium, a demonstration of wit and charm that each of the officers might have liked to make to the young ladies themselves, or might yet make one day. (The daughters of the colonel's elder brother, Count von Z——, they would bring with them not only great prestige but handsome dowries. Matrimony was a traditional shortcut to success in the military.)

"What we must recognize," I remember I suggested, carefully buttering a morsel of roll, "is that love is fundamentally a revolutionary force. It is a threat to the status quo, a disturbance in the present order, with promises of great improvement and risks of great disaster."

The officers listened, not because what I was saying was such a compelling idea but because I spoke with a certain authority. It is for this that I feel to some degree responsible, for I knew what the rumors were that surrounded me. In order to explain my apparent indifference to the charms of some of the local women, certain of my brother officers had speculated that I was a notorious lover, a rakehell, a duelist, a fellow who had arrived at so exquisite a state of ennui that it was no longer the attractiveness of a woman but the skill of her husband or father with pistol or saber that piqued my interest and provided the more irresistible challenge.

I smiled at these stories but corrected none of them. I didn't want to disappoint my friends. I rather enjoyed the mystery with which they had invested my not so fascinating personal history. Most of all, I didn't want to go into the truth of my heritage, which was nobody's business but my own.

"What happens," I said, "is that the Napoleon of today becomes the Napoleon of tomorrow."

There was a scattering of polite laughter. Someone took it upon himself to explain to the nonlaughers what I meant about how the revolutionary officer becomes the conservative emperor, just as the lover becomes the husband.

"The spirit of the Revolution, however, continues, with new partisans appearing all the time, proclaiming Liberty, Equality, Fraternity, and, most of all, Intimacy."

There was no way in which I could have known that Stefan supposed I was speaking to and for him alone, as if I were aware of his extravagances *chez* Krasinska and were encouraging him. Or warning him.

I think I remember his face that evening. We must have noticed each other. There may have been an instant's understanding or misunderstanding, and then I looked elsewhere.

But a part of him must have been answering, Yes, yes, that's exactly my situation. I've gone too far, into depths I could not have imagined. This isn't in my character. I have a more conservative nature than I'd realized. I'm no emperor surely, but a petty burgher, my uncle's nephew after all. I shall go back there, propose marriage to Eugenie, resign my commission, and set up some small business or occupation by which we can support ourselves. It will be inadequate, but it is all I can offer. And Frau Krasinska, recognizing that it is all, will be satisfied or not, will accept me or reject me— and either way I shall be content.

Oblivious to these fevered reflections, I nattered on, "The opposite of war is peace, and the opposite of love is death. And death and peace are both the same in that one seeks them as one also fears them."

Yes, yes, it was all clear to him. He felt as if a weight had been lifted from his heart, and he was all the more grateful because the burden was that of his own guilt. He even was able to look forward to his impending interview with Frau Krasinska with some eagerness instead of dread. He could imagine her relief as he declared himself, her delight as she came to accept her daughter's good fortune.

He was able to drink to the health of the emperor with enthusiasm and even to toast the honor of the regiment without qualification. At the worst, he'd be out soon and its honor would continue unsullied by his brief association as an officer in its service. But he had learned to be wary and was happy enough to be able to get through the afternoon's duties with a relatively clear head and untroubled heart. He would wait to see how his latest resolution fared in the trial of experience. He threw himself into his work, checking and approving surveys that had been made of the region's fords and bridges, and taking a small but meticulous pleasure in the demands of the task. Looking up in amazement to find that the hours had flown, he listed those areas yet to be inspected, signed his report, and passed it on to the colonel's aide. Then he mounted up and began his ride back to face the Krasinskas.

With what wild variations in mood and expectations had he ridden this road! This morning, he had been like a condemned felon on his way to the gallows. Now, he was an honest and upright officer, ready to offer his hand and his honor to restore what he'd arrogated the night before. He rejected the hollow pleasures Captain Kraus was said to pursue, the vainglorious ideas about sexual conquest that were probably fear and bluff more than they were honest reactions to what happens in the world. For Stefan, there was a soothing truth in his recognition that he'd been able at last to make the choice between what they'd been talking about in the regiment and his own actual experience. Yes, of course, it was possible to live the way they all said they lived. But look what came of it! On the other hand, there was the honest life, the authentic emotion of Sonja and Eugenie, into whose home he had come like a criminal, only to be reformed, healed, and made decent again.

He could imagine himself growing old in that house, his hair graying at the temples, his days full of simple but useful tasks and his evenings glowing with familial love. And the nights with Eugenie would be an endless series of rapturous transports. They would move into the front bedroom, perhaps, which was larger. There would be no more of that awful creeping around, on his part or on Sonja's . . . Never? Not even once in a great while? He was no simpleton and could understand that his present high resolve, no matter how sincere, might not be unalloyed with some of the old baser metal, some of the sporty adventurism and the eager curious spirit of experimentation he might one day look back on and associate with his boyhood.

His boyhood. But he was not so much older now than he had been a week before. He had not reached the umbrageous repose of middle age, not quite yet. He could probably find some vestige of his former youthful playfulness if he looked hard enough for it, enough at least to admit to a certain regret at the loss of Sonja's occasional company. Could he give Sonja up? Would he have to, absolutely?

It was as if a cloud had obtruded to darken the route, the day, and his prospects. He was not worthy, and they would know it. They would laugh at him, rejecting his offer with the scorn it deserved. By the time he had installed his horse and set out its mash, he was back to the mood of early that morning, a macerating dejection and an exquisite conviction of his utter worthlessness.

Sonja was waiting for him in the parlor. Eugenie was nowhere to be seen—having been sent away? He stood stiffly in the doorway waiting for the worst.

"Come in," she bade him.

He did so, moved to a distance that was close enough so that she could spit at him if she wanted to, and waited.

"Sit down," she told him.

He did so, but kept his back parade-ground straight.

"We have been discussing our situation, Eugenie and I," she told him. "And I think it is important that all of us understand one another."

"Yes," he said, in much the way he might have told a dentist that he was ready for the extraction to begin.

"What are your . . ."

"Intentions?" he offered.

"In fact, I was about to ask what your feelings are. But I suppose it may amount to the same thing. What are your intentions?"

"To do the right thing," he said.

She laughed. "By whom? For whom?"

"For Eugenie," he said, not at all sure of himself. She was the girl's mother, after all, but she was also a woman in her own right. Whichever way he chose, he'd be offending her. It was an impossible situation. "I am prepared to do whatever is right."

"To marry her?" Sonja asked.

"Yes."

"And do you love her?"

"I shall be devoted to her."

"And faithful?"

"I shall try. I swear it."

"You're absurd, you know. You must realize that your offer is not such a great and noble action as I think you intend. You are willing to bestow upon her your not so enviable hand and tender her your unloving and dutiful heart . . . She won't hear of it. And neither will I."

"You wish me to leave?" he asked. "I shall obey you, whatever your commands." He hardly dared hope for any resolution so simple and painless.

"No, I think not. We have enjoyed your company, Eugenie and I. We shouldn't wish to deprive ourselves of the comfort and protection that come with having a man about the house. Unless you wish to leave, yourself?"

"Not at all," he said, hoping he had hidden his disappointment. He was certain that they had worked out some elaborate punishment, a devious piece of vengeance, and that they would now set its machinery into motion and amuse themselves by watching as it destroyed him.

"Good," she said, smiling, but there was a glint in it.

He asked, partly out of curiosity and partly to demonstrate his boldness, "What is it that you and Eugenie had in mind?"

"You must understand that we are two defenseless women," Sonja began. "We have only each other and this house. A little capital, but then, with the times so uncertain, we cannot rely on that altogether. The point is that we have each other, Eugenie and I. We cannot afford the sentimentality of countesses; we must recognize our position, or, in blunt language, we must know our place. We must not confuse a casual acquaintance like yourself, however amusing, with an ally and a relative."

"I can see that," he said. So far, he saw nothing that was threatening.

"We have agreed, then, that we cannot afford to confuse love and sex either, although the temptation to do so is always very great."

"I agree," he said, mystified but not worried.

"We have further agreed that were either of us to follow one of the impulses that we both share—which is to give you up to the other—we should be jeopardizing our relationship, Eugenie's and mine. Whichever one of us gave you up might resent the other. And whichever one did not give you up might be tempted to fall in love with you—not because of any quality you possess but to justify the sacrifice the other one has made. You see? You understand?"

"I'm not sure I do," he admitted.

"It's not important. The only thing is that you are staying. We shall continue, the three of us, as we have begun."

"We shall stay as we are? We shall just . . . continue?"

"Exactly. It's much the safest thing," Sonja said.

"I can't believe it."

"Can't believe what?"

"My good fortune!"

"But is it so wonderful?"

"I think so," he said. "I'm delighted. I'm more pleased than I can possibly say."

"Eugenie and I are both happy to think so."

"Neither of you wishes to fall in love with me," he said.

"Exactly."

"And so, for the time being at least, we shall simply continue as we have begun."

"What could be more fair to each and to all?" Sonja asked.

"A perfectly intelligent arrangement," he said, praising both of them. "And quite agreeable. I have no words to express my delight in having found the two most civilized women in all of Europe."

PART TWO

XIX · *At the Limits of Fantasy*

It was an unbelievable arrangement, the kind of thing any young man would want if only he had the boldness to imagine it. The two women were not necessarily the most civilized in all of Europe, as Stefan had suggested. Indeed, the thought strikes me that they were, in their provincial backwater, relatively unaffected by the great current of romanticism that had swept over the Continent. They were, therefore, less corrupted, less diminished by the intellectual fashion of the time, so that their native shrewdness was able to operate, that innate cunning by which women and peasants and other powerless but inventive groups have found ways to survive.

Love is a novelty of aristocrats bored with their safe, comfortable lives who yearn for an involvement that carries with it a risk of ruin as well as the prospect of some reward that is otherwise unavailable to them. This cannot be a material reward they can simply buy, haggling for it if need be. Love, the supreme romantic invention, is nonmaterial. And fragile. And it leads, as the librettists have made all too clear, usually to disaster. The disaster is what these aristocrats really long for as an alternative to the ennui, the surfeit, the bloat of their lives. Something worth the risk of disaster will do, but the disaster itself is what beckons.

The middle class, of course, get it all wrong, ape their betters, and crave what they cannot possibly understand. All those decent people, thrifty, industrious, and above all aspiring—and what do they aspire to? World-weariness and the release that the madness of love can offer. It is, depending upon your outlook, either amusing or poignant.

But is it not always so? Invariably, the wrong people dedicate themselves to the particular pastimes for which they have neither the aptitude nor disposition, and sometimes not even the desire. In an effort to remake a self, to redefine or improve it, they hope to effect a change from the outside inward. Or, in a case like Stefan's, they seem to be selected by a whimsical destiny, given opportunities that other men deserve to explore, and ruined, not so much through the richness of the occasion as through the poverty of the resources they bring to it. A modern tragedy, it is the best equivalent our time has to offer to the Attic rituals in which a tragic flaw brought down an otherwise admirable hero. Nowadays, heroic opportunity brings down the common man, and the gods chuckle and smirk, according to their natures and humors.

I do not mean to condescend to Stefan—whom I actually rather liked and of whom I came to be even an admirer, although far too late to do either of us any good. He was a decent fellow, a good-natured young man who, in another role, another time, another set of circumstances, might have found happiness, might even have excelled in some way. There was a nobility in him, deep at the core. There were impurities, too—ambition, fantasy, pretension, and a lack of honesty about his own feelings, but these are by no means unusual. Most of all, there was his youth, his inexperience, which was not at all a matter of talent or breeding, but a passing weakness, a momentary condition. But that was the way he was in his crucial moment. We do not have the choice about these encounters with destiny. It happens in an arbitrary way that we are called to give an account of ourselves, as we are, then and there.

Stefan did not see it in quite that light, of course. Certainly, he would have supposed, at least at first, that he had stumbled into the greatest good fortune any lustful young hussar could imagine, even if he were just spinning stories to go with cards and drinks late at night. An attractive and intelligent young woman and her voluptuous and quite desirable mother alternating as his companions of the night? Who would believe such a thing? But beyond that, there was their refusal to make other demands upon him for any emotional commitment, not to speak of the more mundane and material demands we are accustomed to expect in such circumstances. It was a hussar's heaven.

But the result, curiously enough, was that any lapse from a state of perfect bliss had to be his own fault. He had no one to blame but himself for any discontent he might have felt, any restlessness or dissatisfaction—for which there were, in fact, very reasonable grounds. The open and honest sharing was a strategy the mother and daughter had devised in order to preclude jealousies and rivalries between them. They wanted to resist the temptations to possessiveness that they knew were lurking everywhere in the forest of intimacies into which they had all ventured. The result was that, in an odd way, Stefan felt excluded spiritually even as he was being welcomed physically into their lives. His pride, his self-esteem, his confidence in himself as a fellow worth taking seriously were all at stake, and they were rather more tender than his sturdy physique and facial hair might have suggested.

None of us in the barracks had any idea what was going on, of course. But those of us who liked Stefan, or who took any notice of him, observed a series of subtle changes. The young man who had been outgoing and cheerful at the beginning of his tour of duty with us turned a little quiet, became withdrawn and—we may be forgiven for thinking it—even aloof. In fact, he was lonely, as I can now understand. He had actually lost the feeling of companionship that had begun to develop in the Krasinska household, the opportunities for frank and intimate conversation limited rather than enhanced by the curious sexual arrangement the three of them had devised. And he was, at the same time, cut off from the chance of confiding in his brother officers. He could not

101

seem to boast. He would not have wished to betray the secrets of the Krasinska family and dared not confess that, in an arrangement any of us might envy, he felt lonely and lost. He was turning day by day into something no longer human and seemed to be a kind of object, a toy or a tool. He began to think he was going mad, getting on his gelding every morning to lug his body to the parade ground, and then getting on again at night to take his penis home.

That feeling he had of fragmentation was a reasonable enough reaction to the situation in which they were all denying any possible significance to their nightly wanderings, the way mannerly people at table conspire to deny that they might be hungry, deferring to one another, passing food around, and serving themselves last. He might have been a portion of mashed potatoes, a platter of fried fish, or a revolving relish tray. We, in the barracks, were like another party to the arrangement, as if collectively we amounted to a third woman in this ménage, making demands upon him that were as arbitrary and autocratic as any of theirs. In our defense, I must say that we hadn't known him long enough to be able to judge him or to say with confidence that this withdrawal of his was abnormal or uncharacteristic. Some of us thought his first show of affability had been a manifestation of nervousness that resulted from the novelty of the regiment and the barracks. Once that had worn off, he had returned to a quieter, almost lethargic—one or two even went so far as to suggest stupid—state that was, in fact, his normal condition.

Is that too harsh? It must seem so, I suppose, written that way in letters on a page. But within the regiment, we had a certain tolerance for stupidity. A regiment of hussars is not, after all, a debating club or a philosophers' association. There are worse things to be than stupid. Cowardly, for one. Treacherous. Dishonorable. Many of our best officers were, at their best, rather dull. Still, they had a grace, a dim charm, even a valor that may naturally require for its development an intellectual environment some might consider deprived. It is in the darkest forests that the tallest trees grow, having to force their way upward through the gloom in their quest for light and air.

There was, then, in our judgment about Stefan, no hostility or disesteem, nothing inconsistent with the friendship and affection that ought to obtain among brother officers in a regiment like ours. Otherwise, even though criticism might have been framed, it would never have been uttered aloud.

The closest anyone actually came, I think, was when Lieutenant Biedermeyer suggested that Stefan might be smitten, wounded in some vital spot by one of Cupid's shafts. "You'll see," said Biedermeyer. "It won't last. Either he'll get over it or he'll succeed. In either case, you'll see a transformation of his mood."

"You think it's that simple?" I asked.

"But what else could be bothering him? He's in good health, has the whole world before him, can't have money troubles that we wouldn't know about, doesn't drink to excess. It must be love. Unrequited love, the plague of youth, the very limit of fantasy. I dare say the young woman who is the object of all this adoration doesn't even suspect how the poor creature is dying for a glimpse of her shadow."

"It's possible," I allowed.

"It's inevitable, my dear captain. Inevitable. One goes through it, the way one goes through a trying time of blotchy skin. One outgrows it, thank God."

"I haven't," I told him. "I welcome it. It's so much less trouble than requited love. One doesn't actually have to do anything about it."

"Most of us prefer to do something," Biedermeyer insisted. And then, with a laugh, he said, "But then, most of us aren't as experienced as you are."

"Or as lazy," I said, "which is rather more to the point."

XX · *Brandy or Port*

There was also, for Stefan, a degree of uncertainty that must have been unsettling. To begin with, there was the question of whether he could anticipate the voluptuous embraces of the mother or the angular but more demanding passion of the daughter. But then, some nights, in order to confuse him, to make him worry lest he might have offended, to unnerve him, they left him alone. There would be no invitation, no knock at his door, nothing.

Even that solitude wasn't quite a reprieve, however, for he would lie there in his bed waiting to be summoned, the possibility of action as much a drain on his energies as the action itself—as all military men know who have waited for the drummer or the bugler to sound the attack. He had lost control of his life. Or never having had control, he had lost the comfortable innocence by which he had supposed himself to be autonomous, able to make decisions for himself, or at the very least to express a preference.

It is easy to say that he ought to have known better, should have understood that the decisions were not so great in the first place, that the differences were not so vast between one woman and another. But for those of us who understand these things, there are no words by which we can explain ourselves to others who don't, just as the physician cannot simply explain to his patient what he is doing wrong and how he only has to change from this to that in order to enjoy good health. The patient may know it, intellectually, but be unable to order his body to obey. I remember seeing young

Stefan transfixed—I use the word deliberately, with all its melodrama—by the offer of port or brandy after dinner. He could not choose. It was as if the orderly had presented him a tray with Sonja and Eugenie lying naked, side by side, asking him to pick while the rest of us looked on, indifferently waiting for him to make his selection so that we could get on with our conversation.

He was unable to decide. He actually began to break out in a light sweat. "I . . . I don't know."

"Try the brandy," I prompted. "It's better than usual."

He looked at me in gratitude and relief. "Thank you," he said, and accepted a small pony from the proffered tray.

What a strange fellow, I thought to myself, wondering whether he was not in some way deranged. I smiled at him, as one often smiles at the afflicted, to ward off the evil eye, placate the disadvantaged, disarm the animosity of the potentially dangerous deviant, and also in some small measure to show sympathy. He took my smile the wrong way, of course, interpreting it as an invitation to conversation, the very last thing in the world I had in mind.

XXI · *An Honest Involvement*

It would be tedious to recreate—as it was tedious to endure in the first place—the recitation by Stefan of the steps of his journey from innocence and tranquility to the perturbation in which he now found himself. He did not come forth with his story in one long session of confession but made little forays, like some tiny animal driven and at the same time terrified, darting forward and scampering back, each time testing me to see whether I was paying attention or, even more particularly, to determine what kind of attention I was paying. I take no credit for having been mildly bored, but that was what he required. He needed someone who did not react much to the revelations he thought were incredible, salacious, depraved, and nearly bestial. I listened politely enough, but without any suggestion of incredulity or shock. That was what he found and, evidently, exactly what he required.

I expected him to ask me for advice, mostly because that was usually the result of these confessions—of which I must admit I had heard more than my share during the course of my career. I think there must be some peculiarity of my physiognomy that suggests I am sympathetic and approachable. If I could determine what that peculiarity was, I could have it corrected and should thereby save my fellow officers a good deal of wasted breath and effort. Still, I listened, waiting for some request for a strategic suggestion or, even worse, a demand for a loan, but all Stefan wanted was the assurance that he was not a monster. He had fucked the woman and then had fucked her daughter, was still fucking them both and enjoying it, and yet he felt absolutely miserable. I found, despite myself, that I was beginning to be interested in the young man, as a naturalist is interested in an unusual specimen. He was a product of our middle-class culture, the end result of all the publicly professed ideals and morals upon which the empire proclaims itself to be built, and in defense of which its might and majesty are ever ready to exert themselves.

"Why," I asked him, "do you consider yourself to be more of a monster than either of them? Why is it necessary that you be the exploiting one and that they be the victims? Why isn't it just as accurate to exchange the labels? Or discard them altogether? Why must there be a victim at all? Is anyone forcing anyone to do anything?"

"But that's just it," he replied. "No one is forcing me. I could have refused. I could refuse, now, tonight. But I won't. I am like a drunk who craves the liquor he knows he cannot handle. I am terrified by it but drawn to it, fascinated and helpless."

"Nonsense."

"Yes, isn't it? It's the absence of sense, sheer irrationality! I am no longer a rational human being, and that's what is bestial. That is the very nature of being a beast."

"If you insist," I said. "But in that case, we are most of us beasts. Either beasts or corpses."

"Your amused attitude would be appropriate if I were enjoying myself, but I'm not. I feel lonely and adrift, on a great philosophical ocean . . ."

"Nonsense! You are indulging in excessive metaphors."

That shut him up for a while, as it was clearly intended to do. My patience with this kind of exchange was limited. Still, I found myself later on considering his predicament, one that most young men would find desirable but to which he was not at all suited. Were there ways in which I could change his mind, or rearrange his emotional and philosophical underpinnings so that he could allow himself to enjoy what the fates had so generously offered him? It was an undertaking all the more objective and scientific in that I did not particularly like Stefan, was not especially drawn to him, was in fact mildly annoyed by his inability to delight in what was so marvelous a circumstance. He was irksome, the way a child can sometimes be irksome when he refuses to try a new food. One pleads with the child, reassures him, then loses patience and bullies.

I was tempted to bully Stefan, to turn against him the very fears he had admitted to me—about the possible scorn of his fellow officers, the contemptuous laughter he felt might at any moment sound forth, mocking him as he was secretly convinced he deserved to be mocked. But what an achievement it would be, I thought, if I could listen to him, let him talk his way around the problem, and prod him toward some better understanding and adjustment, either to a choice between the two women or to an accommodation to the gift of both their favors. That seemed to me the ideal outcome, and in order to accomplish it, I forced myself to be available, to show a modicum of friendliness, at least a willingness to endure his breast-beatings, his self-indulgent recitation of trivial details, his self-dramatizations. I told myself it was for science, for the disinterested experiment the project offered, but I was fooling myself as surely as he was himself. It was not until much later that I realized there was something in this configuration that spoke to me with the siren's voice, some alluring message that was meant only for me. The young lieutenant had no idea, and I had no realization of it either at the beginning. But there it was, the mother and the daughter together, outcasts, allies, fending for themselves, using their bodies and wits to try to make a life for themselves—just as my mother and grandmother had done.

I had noticed the daughter's name was Eugenie, which is not a common name in this part of the world. Could it have some private significance? Had Herr Krasinski been away on a trip somewhere, and had Frau Krasinska perhaps found a substitute for him in her bed? Had Eugenie been better born than her mother's husband suspected? I did not know the truth, but was free to assume what I liked. And clearly it pleased me to imagine a coincidence between these two women I had never met and my own family, my own history, my own disreputably noble lineage. Not that I supposed Eugenie might also carry Hapsburg blood, which is not at all important. But the pretension, the dissatisfaction with the world as it is, the restlessness, and the inability to settle for life as we find it . . . all those things I think of in association with largeness of soul.

For their sakes, it was important that I try to rehabilitate and improve this miserable specimen. But in the end, I came to recognize that it was for my sake, my own sake, as it ought to be if we are ever serious about our actions. Anything else, however convincingly it may masquerade as altruism, is meddling, trifling with other people's lives, and dishonest. My involvement was honest and fundamental, but as with so many important impulses, I had at the time no understanding of why and how this was so. I listened to Stefan's recitations, showed him patience and courtesy beyond anything a saint might be expected to manifest, and found myself the object of an adoration that would have made most angels blush.

XXII · *A Simple Suggestion*

The problem, as I understood it, was that Stefan felt himself to be shut out emotionally even if he was made welcome physically by the Krasinskas, whom he suspected of some sort of conspiracy. "It is unnatural," he insisted, "how they are so close. They are readier to confide in each other than in me."

"But what could be more normal?" I asked him. "Remember, they are not rivals. They are mother and daughter, the most natural allies. They have known each other forever, and you are the newcomer, the intruder. They are right to keep you from separating them, from pitting one against the other. And you are quite wrong to take their bonds of affection and understanding as any kind of challenge."

Giving advice is easy. I watched him struggle for a moment, fail, and then reject it. "All that may be true," he said. "I still feel lonely there, isolated. An outsider."

"As you well might. You are the outsider, relatively speaking. The trouble may be that you are too importunate. They will be more forthcoming if you are less so. Have you never made friends with a strange dog? You don't pursue the animal. It only makes him suspicious or shy. You stand still, extend your hand perhaps, and allow the dog to come to you. It will sidle up, sniff your hand, then lick it. And in five minutes it will be rolling on the ground before you, inviting you to scratch its stomach."

"You think that would work?" he asked.

"Something like that, yes. Don't always be the pursuer. Let them come to you."

Again, I watched him thinking about it. This time, he did not reject the idea, but from his furrowed brow I could see that he was troubled. "Well?" I prompted. "What's the difficulty?"

"They'll never believe it. They'll know I'm only pretending."

"But will they? Are they not pretending to you? Don't they have each other to help in the pretense? Do you suppose they are absolutely sure of themselves and that you are the only one with doubts and inadequacies? Or are they not also mere humans, susceptible to all the uncertainties you and I experience all the time?"

He was thinking.

"Isn't that why they stick together so tightly, relying upon each other? Isn't it just possibly a sign of the very weakness you feel, yourself? Think, man. Be reasonable! Be fair, not only to yourself, but to them, too. You ought to admire how well they've done, thus far, and you can't do that if you begin with the assumption that they are superhuman creatures who only deign to walk on the earth because it would be vulgar to float in the air where they might call attention to themselves."

He realized it was a joke, smiled, and then laughed. He wasn't altogether hopeless. "Yes, I see what you mean," he finally admitted. "All right, I'll try it."

"Splendid," I said, lighting a postprandial cigar.

"How do I do that?"

"Just think of the dog. Let them come to you. Take a book home, for one thing. Read. Better yet, absent yourself from time to time. Let them wonder when you are coming home. Don't be so tiresomely reliable. You can stay here some evenings and play cards. Or you can find work to do of some sort. We do so little, after all, and keep it a mystery. People out in the world have no idea what our duties are. You could always claim to have some pressing task. Not every night, mind you. But on occasion. Let them long for you a little. Let them feel impatience. Let them even learn to compete for your time, which they might do if you spent less time there."

111

"Yes, yes, I see."

"Let me know how it goes," I told him. Even now, as I write that sentence, I shudder to think how innocent it seems. As it seemed then. An expression of mere good manners? A brother officer's friendliness? Yes, it was that kind of nearly empty phrase. But there I was, having made a suggestion, having offered a prescription. And it wasn't because I am such a helpful, friendly, and sympathetic chum, either. On the contrary, I had thought simply to get rid of the youngster, to shut him up. But there was also my envy of his passion, my recognition that he was burning with a desire, not merely for the women's bodies (which he could enjoy at their whim but still often enough), but for their submission, their spiritual yielding. It was foreign to me to care about anything or anyone with such intensity. It was also my idle notion that if he were to redress what he perceived to be an imbalance, then his thirst for them might be slaked and his passion satisfied, even sated. I could, by this manipulation, reduce him to my own condition of elegant ennui, and promote him an entire social class.

By way of exculpation, I must say that this was not my only thought, or even, at the instant of our conversation, my uppermost concern. But it was there, creeping into my mind in an odd moment, now and again, when I passed the young lieutenant on the parade ground and saw the way he seemed preoccupied, caught up by the thrill of his position with the Krasinska women, like a small boy up in a tree, afraid to descend, afraid to move higher, but aware that he cannot rest forever in that comfortable crotch in which he has temporarily found a perch.

XXIII · *A Correction and an Invitation*

I have often imagined how it must have been: an unremarkable scene, with each of the actors trying not to be awkward and not to react to the artificiality of the others. But each of them would have been keyed up, alerted by some subtle change in the atmosphere. Stefan, for example, would have been sitting up late in the parlor, reading a text on military strategy, perhaps Maine's *Infantry Fire Tactics,* or Prince Kraft's *Letters on Infantry, Cavalry, and Artillery.* Upstairs, in their rooms, Eugenie and Sonja would have been in bed, pretending to read but waiting to hear the sound of Stefan's boots on the staircase, the noise of running water in the bathroom, the diffident rap upon a door.

But nothing! There would then have been a slow blossoming of concern, first for themselves, then for each other, and then, in the creeping minutes, a reconsideration of their relative tactical positions. Had they taken him for granted? Had they assumed too much? Was he simply tired this evening or was this a sign of a more general fatigue? Had he already begun to be bored with them? And how did they feel about that? Could he be replaced, or had they, perhaps, outmaneuvered themselves, so that they had more of an investment in him than they had intended or supposed?

Each of them, in her room, in her own way and at her own pace, would have taken these emotional and intellectual hurdles, trying to imagine the very worst possibility—as one does in such a situation—and then finding permutations that were still worse.

There was probably no such single moment, no one evening when the waves of awareness broke upon their several heads, his downstairs in the pool of lamplight, and theirs upstairs in the softer glow of the single candles each had placed upon her nightstand. Instead, over the course of a week or two, a gradual realization would have come to them of the shifting in the emotional balance. That it was a feigned change makes no difference. The ability to feign was enough, the capacity to pretend and premeditate, which Stefan had not been able to manage before, was an unimpeachable sign of a new relationship.

Even the sex would have changed, a vehicle now for different feelings entirely. Eugenie, in particular, would have felt—and certainly would have shown—her insecurity and her desire somehow to hang on to the young hussar whom fate had dropped into her life and lap. Stefan, noticing her new expenditure of extra effort, a novel energy and zest, would have been flattered, pleased with himself, and encouraged to continue his show of indifference or at least the self-contained poise that had elicited from her these wonderful demonstrations of eager welcome. Compared to the Eugenie of this period, Sonja must have seemed almost dull, offering her confident efficiency in an encounter that was almost like an athletic exercise in which two companions enjoy each other's company as they work out together.

But he could not simply diminish his visits with Sonja and increase his moments of pleasure with Eugenie. They were exchanging this kind of information, or so Stefan assumed. It was absence and abstinence that he would have had to use as his medium of expression, just at the very moment when Eugenie's uncertainty made her so much more ardent and appealing.

With all the contradictory communication, that tangle of cross-purposes and mixed motives, there would have been a peculiarly dramatic stillness as the three of them pretended to read, one downstairs and the two others up in their respective bedrooms, each thinking of the others with a vividness and focus that would have been impossible had the others been present. I can imagine Eugenie pining for Stefan; Sonja fretting for Eugenie's unhappiness; Stefan fighting off the temptations of lust for the sake of his own refined taste and the possibilities of its greater satisfaction. He must have contemplated Eugenie, and Sonja, and the fundamental unpredictability and irrationality of sex, about which he was rapidly becoming a philosopher.

He also was getting to be fairly well read, for a young lieutenant, in the classics of military strategy. Some of those pages he had read six or eight times, and their meaning had begun to sink in.

He reported back to me, not all the physical details, of course—those he left me to infer—but the new emotional topography. That was his word, picked up, I think, from Prince Kraft's *Letters.* He had managed to take and hold the bluff, as it were. And he now commanded a fair piece of the field. But what should his next move be? How ought he to proceed?

"That depends," I told him, "on what you want. You have to decide what your objective is." I had reached the very same conclusion as had his own batman.

Or, not quite the same. Stefan, himself, had gone beyond that earlier impasse. "I know what I want," he said. "I want Eugenie to love me."

"Eugenie, and not the mother?"

"That's right."

"What about you? Do you love her?" I asked. We sounded rather like schoolgirls, but how else can one talk of such matters?

"I think so. I think of her all the time. I think of how impossible it is . . ."

"Impossible? What are you talking about? You can go to her room anytime you want. You've been fucking her for a month . . ."

"But that's just it. I want to go back to the beginning and start over. I want to erase everything that has happened. This

115

business of having had her mother as well as Eugenie just ruins everything. We can never have a normal relationship. It can't ever be the way it's supposed to."

"But who supposes? Where are you getting these crazy rules of yours? Can't you just accept what you have and delight in it? It seems attractive enough to me. It's what you thought you wanted, yourself, a month ago. It's exactly what you hoped for."

"I was wrong."

"And now you're right? This is wisdom?"

"She's a sweet girl. She deserves better than this."

"You're absurd," I told him, having lost patience to such an extent that I actually said what I was thinking. He did not take it well. Rather stiffly, but with as much dignity as his years and rank could carry, he excused himself and wished me a "good afternoon," *à l'anglaise,* in which icy usage it aspires to be a withering remark.

I was annoyed, of course, with him but with myself, too. Why did it matter? What was the point of my feeling anything, let alone feeling it sharply enough to betray impatience? I was a senior officer, and this youngster, almost a boy really, had come to me with his problems. I had tried to listen to him but had wearied and had made light of them and of him, too. It took me an hour or so to realize I'd been wrong, and another to begin to feel the chagrin that comes from having behaved badly. Only later did it occur to me to wonder why I had done so, or what it was about Stefan's story, however absurd, that had grated on me, touching some raw nerve somewhere.

I resolved, at any rate, to make it up to him somehow. I stopped him the next day, apologized—a thing I almost never do—and inquired how he was getting on.

"Well enough," he said, cautious after my earlier attack.

"Good," I told him. "I'm glad to hear it." I realized that it is not so easy a thing to do as I had believed when I told him how to stand still and let them come to him. I had to do the same now, with him, letting him come to me in his own good time. I told myself that when he had a question, he would come to me with it, inasmuch as I was the one to whom he had unburdened himself in the first place. The choice was between me and another officer, to whom he would have to tell all, beginning at the beginning and risking rejection and ridicule. I had listened, after all, to a fair amount of his confession already. Sooner or later, he'd be prompted to resume our conversation.

It turned out to be sooner, and with some real cause. I had not reckoned on his incredible luck. Apparently, all he needed to do was to express a desire and the world conformed to his wishes, as if to demonstrate to him how little difference it made and show him that he could design his own torments as efficiently as could any blind fate. He had declared himself as Eugenie's lover, and had expressed some chagrin about his connection with her mother. As if with a magic wand, or through some less suggestive instrumentality, there was a transformation. The daughter had confided in her mother that she was smitten, adored Stefan, and was worried about his lack of an ardent commitment to her. The mother considered the problem and decided to withdraw from the arrangement, leaving the two youngsters to find their way through the thickets of love, either to a grand passion or to some escape. Upon his return to the Krasinska house that evening, the two women had confronted him in the parlor and had more or less commanded him to join them in a conference. "We have to discuss our situation," Sonja informed him.

He thought of resisting, imagined issuing a lofty refusal, but could not bring himself to do so. Instead, he seated himself and looked attentive, trying to avoid any show of nervousness such as a twitch or an idiotic grin, the irrational fear of which is sometimes overwhelming in grave moments. "I was convinced," the young man told me, "that they had decided together to end the arrangement, that it was despicable and beastly, and that, somehow, they had contrived a way to blame me for everything. I remember feeling the unfairness of it as I waited for what I felt sure was going to be a moralized tirade."

"And?" I asked.

"And there was nothing of the kind. The mother asked me if I was unhappy or dissatisfied in any way."

"You told her the truth?"

What the lieutenant told her was that he was "uneasy" and "apprehensive." He was not as forthcoming as he might have been. Perhaps it was a failure of nerve. He did not say that he felt excluded, even that he was being used, was being turned into a plaything, an object. Not having the wish to offend them or the necessary sternness of character to force them to take responsibility for what they had done, he converted that first irrational fear—that they would blame him for what had happened—into an obligation of decency and good manners.

"We have been seeing rather less of you," the mother chided.

"I have been unavoidably occupied by regimental duties," he said, a polite fiction no one was obliged to believe.

"Eugenie is concerned about it. Indeed, I might even say she is upset," Sonja continued.

"I'm sorry, indeed, to hear it."

"Are you?" Sonja asked.

"Certainly," Stefan insisted, not happy to have his word challenged.

"Perhaps you are. But are you not also secretly pleased? Flattered maybe? Are you not just a little proud of yourself for having wrung from her—from us—such an admission? Does it not gratify you to know that, in her way, she cares for you?"

"I am delighted to hear that, of course."

"And your feelings for her?"

"I'm not sure," he said, either honest or shrewd. He didn't know which, himself. "I find myself . . . confused."

"Yes, I can understand that. It is what we had supposed. It is perhaps why you have been avoiding us."

"I really have been occupied," he maintained.

"So you really may have believed. Still, the effect has been the same, has it not?" Sonja asked.

"It's nothing to be ashamed of," Eugenie prompted.

"Possibly. I don't know," he said. He could admit to anything as a possibility, just so long as he wasn't tied to it and didn't have to answer for it. But there would be answerability, one way or another, waiting to grab him. He was sure of that.

"We're not trying to trap you," Sonja said, as if she could read his mind. This was not altogether reassuring.

"It's all right, Stefan. Believe me!" Eugenie promised. He was still not reassured.

"I think . . . Or, I should say that we think, for we have discussed it together . . . it might be better all around if I were to disengage myself, to withdraw from the pleasant arrangement into which we seem to have drifted. At least for a time. That way, the two of you will have some opportunity to discover whether you are more comfortable in each other's company and what sort of future you have together—if any. To come to know your own minds and hearts, without any distraction or complication. Do you agree?"

"Yes," he said, trying not to sound too eager lest Sonja be offended. What incredible good fortune! What a pair of understanding women! It was what he had hoped to engineer and had decided was impossible, but here they were handing it to him on a platter. "Yes, I think that's a perfectly reasonable suggestion."

"Not that you would be committed in any way," Eugenie said. "I shouldn't like that. It has to be a spontaneous relationship, free on both sides, or it can't be anything at all, at least as far as I am concerned."

"I've always admired your freedom of spirit," Stefan said. It was too good to be true. He kept thinking that there must be a catch somewhere, some equivalent disadvantage, some burden, but try as he might he was unable to find it. Still, he felt apprehensive.

"If you'll excuse me, then," Sonja said, "I'll be going on up to bed. I wish you both a good night."

"And she went upstairs, leaving us alone, together," Stefan told me. "It seemed obligatory, then, for me to accompany Eugenie to her room, and, despite what she'd said about freedom, just as obligatory for me to spend the night with her—which is something I'd never done before. I mean, we'd slept together and done all the things people do in bed, but I'd never spent the whole night and awakened with her in the morning. It felt as though we were married, which is just what she said we weren't to feel. But there it was, that very feeling."

"I can understand that," I said.

"What should I have done? What should I do now?"

"It does no good to think about what you should have done. That can't be changed. The only question is what you ought to do now. What do you want to do?"

"I think I want to continue as I am, at least for the present. I think it's just what I wanted."

"And what you still want?"

"I think so," he said, but he didn't sound altogether sure. There was a pause, and then he suggested, "Perhaps you might come out one Saturday afternoon to join us for a meal. You might have more to go on for the purposes of forming an opinion and giving advice—that is if you don't mind—if you were to meet these women. They are very pleasant, very interesting . . ."

"Oh, I have no doubt of that," I told him.

"If it's convenient, of course . . ."

He wasn't going to force it. Or plead with me. Or make any clearer the idea that Sonja was available and that it might be decent of him to provide a substitute lover for her. But if I was interested, he'd made the suggestion, to which I could respond however I liked.

"We'll see," I said. "Let me think about it."

XXIV · *Old Acquaintance*

What I discovered was something Stefan had already told me but which I'd overlooked, either unwilling or unable to accommodate it to the categories I'd prepared over the years. When I went out there—as of course I was bound to do, sooner or later, if only to get it over with—what struck me was Eugenie's foot.

No, she did not kick me, but the situation did, the specificity of it, the poignance, the ineluctability of her defect. I saw at once not only her odd rolling gait but the effect it must have had upon Stefan, its vivid demonstration of love's debility. Let us agree that love is an ailment, a crippling wound or an impairment of some analogous kind, and let us also grant that among decent people both male and female, there can come, along with passion and one's crafty efforts to engineer a reciprocal passion in the object of one's love, a sympathy, a pity even, that is the result of one's understanding of how the beloved is losing or has lost poise, independence, and the ability to stand—it crossed my mind in these terms—alone, and on his or her own two feet. The French say that one has been *bouleversé,* knocked over by *amour,* and it is indeed a staggering experience. The girl, then, with her limp, seemed not only an example but the very emblem of the suffering Stefan was himself experiencing and requiring of her.

If I am not presuming too far, I believe I also saw—or ought to have seen?—another curious manifestation of the madness of love, an awkwardness that often presents itself to sensitive souls as they go about the work of conforming their experience to their expectations. Stefan was exactly that kind of sensitive youth, and while his ideas about love may have been acquired haphazardly and may not have had much subtlety, they were very vivid in his mind because they had not yet been smudged and aged by use. He knew that a mistress was supposed to be proud and imperious, a worthy object of veneration, an almost unapproachable figure more at home in dream or legend than in the ordinary world accessible to anyone. Eugenie was not unapproachable at all, had given herself freely (with perhaps a spiritual grandeur and pride, but still not according to the conventions), and she seemed to be a conquered bastion, and in that way an object of his condescension.

Those reflections all came to me rather later, I must admit. What occupied me at the moment of my arrival were more immediate concerns. I was looking at the house, the style of the furnishings, the quality of the women, making the kind of quick appraisal that is accurate because it is heartless and is impossible after the first ten minutes or so. I was doing this for my own amusement as much as on behalf of my fellow officer in whose life I had accepted a commission to meddle. The widow was a woman of more sophistication than I might have expected way out in Waldenburg, well put together and intelligently dressed. She knew how to make the best of herself without calling attention to her artifice. And she had probably been her daughter's consultant if not just her teacher. The younger one was turned out in a frilly garment that seemed just a touch frivolous at first but then had its effect by underscoring and framing her fundamental seriousness. It was a bold but successful gesture. Good books on the shelves, and the pictures on the walls were not the usual prints and copies but showed some originality of taste, even some eccentricity. Comfortable rooms, if a bit fussy. My impression, even before spending any time in conversation, was that these were estimable women who might have had perfectly reasonable lives in one or another of the capital cities of Europe. Whether happy or not is, naturally, another question, but perfectly reasonable, indistinguishable from any other comparable pair in Bucharest or Budapest or even Vienna or Paris.

Certainly, Stefan had not discredited himself or the regiment. He was in no way jeopardizing his own or our collective respectability. I remember thinking that, and then seeing her, a few moments later, cross the room to ring for the servant to bring tea. That gait and her defective foot were all at once clear to me. But how foolish, how fortuitous and factitious a detail to bother about! If that was their only problem, he had nothing to worry about, no cause for uncertainty or self-consciousness. I was relieved at how simple the answer was. All I had to do was tell him, straight out and in such a way as to be convincing, and he could have his chance at whatever it was the gods of love and war had in their cupboards with which to tempt or threaten him.

The old woman he'd mentioned they had as a servant came in to answer Eugenie's summons. "Wanda, would you bring in the samovar?"

"Certainly, mademoiselle."

I recognized the voice first, then the face. Wanda? Not my old Wanda, from the days of my youth! Was it possible? I did some rapid calculation. Back then, when I was fifteen or sixteen, she would have been in her early forties perhaps. And now, twenty years later? It was not to be excluded absolutely, but what a falling off! Her teeth were mostly gone, which gave her a facial expression of enormous age. And she had put on weight, maybe to make up for those many years of being careful about her diet to preserve her looks. But, yes, there was something familiar about the eyes and a way she had of holding her head.

"Wanda? Is that you?" I asked.

She looked at me, squinted, came closer, grinned, and then laughed. "The young master," she said. And she came to me and gave me a hug.

"How wonderful to see you," I said. And I explained to Frau Krasinska and her daughter, as well as to Stefan, "She used to work for my mother and grandmother, back in Vienna, many years ago."

"I'll get the samovar," she said.

XXV · *Wanda Confides*

Stefan, meanwhile, was beside himself with nervousness. He had engineered this meeting for a number of intricately mixed motives he had not properly sorted out. Surely he hadn't decided what he wanted to happen, or feared might happen, or even hoped to discover. It was as if the uncertainties of inactivity and the need for patience were themselves driving him toward relief or disaster, either of which would be welcome. He wanted me to approve of Eugenie. That was clear. He wanted me to approve of Sonja, as well. Or, I should say, of Sonja even more particularly. I had the not so idle thought that I was perhaps to be his replacement in that quarter. But it could not appear to Sonja that he had consciously arranged such a thing. Stefan did not want to be seen to be pandering for her. It was, I am sure, a mark of his delicacy and tact, although the effect was rather less refined. Indeed, it was my impression that Sonja began to perceive how some of his perturbation arose from his worries about how he'd treated her. Instead of diverting attention from the possible awkwardness or simply ignoring it, he was in effect calling it to everyone's attention. He was therefore flustered and however hard he tried to seem relaxed and at ease, he failed so miserably that the rest of us found it difficult to maintain among ourselves a surface of civilized affability.

There was little I could to to calm him or help us all get through the awkwardness we were feeling, because I was its occasion. I could make myself scarce, however, and let them find their balance again. I excused myself to go off to the kitchen and renew my acquaintance with Wanda, one of the companions and tutors my grandmother had provided me during those delightful days of my adolescence.

"Master Rudolph," she said, using my first name, now that we were alone. "You're looking very grand."

"And you, Wanda, are looking wonderful. In good health, I trust?"

"If I'd had lovers as attentive as the aches and pains that pursue me now, I'd have had a fine life indeed. But I shouldn't complain. To feel anything at all is better than the alternative, is it not?"

"As you once taught me."

"You remember," she said, grinning. It wasn't a question.

"With rapture," I told her, truthfully. It had been she who had first trained me in the art of amatory endurance, letting me lie motionless for hours, balancing and refining the sensitivity of my nerves so that I could learn how my body worked and how it could be an instrument of pleasure not only for myself but for another as well. *Carezza*, the Italians call it—unless they use a French name for it.

"You always were a sweet boy," she said.

"I was an eager pupil," I replied.

"Yes, that you were," she agreed.

I asked her about Frau Krasinska and her daughter. What could she tell me about them?

"They are what they seem, or very nearly. What would you like to know?"

"About Krasinski—Eugenie's father," I said, taking a shot in the dark or, at least, deep gloom. There was the tantalizing hint of her name, after all.

"Ah, but which one?" Wanda asked.

"Both of them," I said.

Almost certainly, Eugenie's real father was a Radziwill who had been Bishop of Breslau some twenty years before. A wonderful passionate affair it had been, too, with the young madame thinking herself the worst woman in the world, the devil's own temptress, as wicked as Eve, bringing down the soul of the holy man and plunging him into the fiery pit. And, of course, she loved it, because she knew she was worth an eternity of suffering, as the bishop's attentions reaffirmed at each meeting when she would come in through the secret entrance to the episcopal palace—not stopping to wonder what such an entrance could have been designed and built for except such visits.

And then, she came up pregnant, as so often happens in these sad stories. "But the bishop was better than most," Wanda told me, "arranging the marriage to Krasinski and officiating at the baptism of his daughter, giving her the name of Eugenie and other gifts as well."

"This Krasinski? A relative of the poet, perhaps?"

"A distant cousin, it was said, but that may have been a hope only."

"What sort of fellow was he?"

"Oh, very nice," Wanda said, looking down at her shoes. "Very nice, indeed."

"But?"

"He preferred boys, I believe. It was a marriage of mutual convenience. He had a wife and the possibility of an heir to carry on his name. She had a father for her child. The bishop had arranged the matter to everyone's satisfaction, don't you see? It was advantageous all around."

"What happened, then?"

"They lived happily ever after, as the saying goes. Until the husband died. They became fond of each other, actually. I came into their service a year or so before he died. He was quiet and sweet, and loved the little girl as if she were his own. It was a shame he was taken off that way."

"Interesting," I said, thinking that I had more in common with them than with Stefan. Or that, conversely, they had more in common with me than with the callow lieutenant. What were they bothering with him for? Why all these voluptuary delights should be wasted on that fellow was a question irrational to ask and annoying to answer. Could it be simply that he had been assigned here in the randomness of the billeting arrangements? The truth of it could not have been more obvious or irksome.

And yet, I suppose, if I were in their place, I could see a certain advantage to him, his youth, his inexperience, his harmlessness, all worth practicing on, all recommending themselves as the ideal beginner's slope whereon the novice might acquire the knack of downhill skiing. The girl, just starting out, and the mother, idly amusing herself one more time, perhaps not the last time but with such a possibility always before her . . . They might well have settled upon him as a suitable candidate, particularly if they joined forces to keep him manageable and docile. The more I thought of it, reviewing and reordering those pieces of information I had gleaned from Stefan's meandering confessions, the more reasonable it seemed to me. The simple truth of it was that he was a mere preliminary for a main event that was to follow, an overture before the first grand scene. In some way or other, with a clear-eyed wisdom only women possess, they had been preparing themselves for the entrance of a worthy protagonist for their fantasies.

I caught myself. I could not be that protagonist, however appealing the role might be. I was prohibited by my connection with Stefan as a friend and brother officer. The mother, perhaps, might be a diversion for me, or the other way around, but to come in and play the complicated double-stopped score they had been composing was not my destiny. A pity, but then life is full of tantalizations and disappointments.

"And you?" I asked, recalling myself to duty. "How has the world treated you?" I asked Wanda. "You seem content."

"I have my great love, which is food. And I have a comfortable home. They are not fussy. Neither are they so indulgent as to be insulting to me. I learned to keep house to a certain standard in your mother's service, after all. I am as good a cook as one can find in the town of Waldenburg."

"You were always talented at whatever you put your hand to," I told her.

"You were always a naughty boy. But, please, do me a favor. You must not speak a word of this to the lieutenant."

"Of Eugenie's lineage? He doesn't know?"

"I don't think so. It's up to her to tell him or not. I shouldn't like to presume. I'd never have told you except that we go back so far and know each other so well."

"I won't say a word, I promise." I couldn't help wondering why she wanted to keep it a secret. Might she be afraid of scaring him off? Could a connection, however unofficial, with the princely family of Radziwill intimidate him that way?

On the other hand, I never spoke about my Hapsburg blood. I didn't like the feeling of boasting. Or of confirming the obvious. With my little Hapsburg jaw, I was obviously related either to a family of rabbits or to the Hapsburgs, and since I didn't have long furry ears, the royal family was the likelier bet.

Eugenie, fortunately, had been spared the Radziwill nose. A pretty young thing, she was . . .

I caught myself again. Have a care!

Twice in five minutes?

I promised myself I'd be a perfect gentleman, get through the afternoon, and beat a dignified retreat. Back to the barracks and the brandy bottle, and let Stefan struggle as he might to keep from smothering in the soft down of the Krasinska comforters.

XXVI · *The Rewards of Gallantry*

I returned to the living room ready to endure the awkwardness for as long as good manners required, but the mood had somehow changed. It could have been that my expectations were now so low that anything other than torment was a pleasant surprise. Or, more probably, it could have been some subtle exchange whereby my attitude toward them communicated itself, my intentions to the contrary notwithstanding. Stefan intuited my envy of his fortunate position, felt complimented by it, and was happy to have the one assurance he could trust that I approved of his young lady. Eugenie sensed—as women are often able to do—the rivalry between us, however repressed and disguised. It made her blossom, put her at her ease, and allowed her to pose as if in a hall of mirrors, every attitude doubling and redoubling to an infinity of complicated reflections. Sonja, meanwhile, no longer the center of attention in the sordid transaction she must have suspected, could now relax, allow her daughter the fun and glamour, and content herself—as she had been content before—with whatever scraps fell from that abundant feast.

There was talk of poetry and the theater, about the latest fashions in Paris and Vienna, and of course about love and death, the risks of the military career. There was wine and there were little cakes Eugenie passed around—to demonstrate that she could perform such tasks without mishap. There was a simple cold supper, or that's what Sonja announced. I recognized the squab in aspic from my childhood. Wanda had spent hours preparing it, enjoying herself no doubt, just as I enjoyed eating again a dish my grandmother had taught her to prepare. A Hapsburg's gift to the Radziwills, but I could not publish the observation, having promised Wanda not to betray the confidence. It was not at any rate a secret that I wanted to share. I delighted in knowing something Stefan didn't, in having a grasp of the situation he didn't have, a proprietorship even.

There were things he knew that I didn't, but those were ordinary things anyone could guess. I could look at Eugenie and extrapolate from the tiny hairs of her neck what the small of her back might look like. I could transpose her laugh, high and birdlike, and imagine what her cries of passion might sound like. I could watch her lips as she nibbled a *petit four* and hazard a guess as to what her kisses would feel like. Or I could catch a glimpse of Sonja's delight in her daughter's pleasure and from that datum leap to an understanding of how Stefan had found himself in this extraordinary situation in this backwater town.

It was immediately apparent to me, for example, that he owed his spectacular success as much to her clubfoot as to any quality of his own. Another mother of another child might have been more cautious, more protective. But this mother, considering the disadvantage her daughter needed to overcome, was willing to take greater risks. Or, more simply, she was unwilling to be overprotective, wanting the girl to live life as well and as completely as the limitations of the town, the times, her fortune, and her foot permitted. Either way, I found myself agreeing with the mother and approving of her attitude. Exactly right, I thought. And yet, to Stefan, they were merely eccentric and depraved, beyond his comprehension and therefore beyond his ability to trust them. He kept looking for mean and believable explanations that were unworthy of these women.

The afternoon nevertheless went well. Stefan basked in my approval and was able to delight in Eugenie, to be proud of her and answer her jokes and flights of fancy with his own clever remarks, for he was by no means stupid but only innocent. I was the appreciative audience for whom they were all eager to perform well, to be just a little better than on an average day. I even found a kind of satisfaction in the thought that such appreciation is just what most of us need to tip the scales in our lives from not quite satisfactory to some positive reading. Self-regard is the first step toward salvation.

At last, the shadows began to lengthen. I suggested that it was time for me to take my leave. Stefan offered to ride back to the barracks with me. I assured him I could find my way easily enough, and he was confident enough of my approbation that he was able to let me ride off, thereby postponing our inevitable analysis until the following day.

On the way back, I had the idle thought that if, somehow, Stefan were to meet with an accident, be thrown from his horse and hit his head on an outcropping of rock, say, then I might renew my acquaintance with Frau Krasinska and her charming daughter. But absent such an untoward circumstance, I decided I had better forget about them both.

I did tell Stefan, the next day, that I thought his young lady was wonderful and her mother was also remarkable. The young lieutenant cross-examined me, as if I were a hostile witness, trying to shake my testimony that he feared to trust. I assured him I was not being polite, that I truly admired both of them, envied him, and had even imagined his death so that I could contrive to take his comfortable place in the billeting arrangements. He believed that and let me alone.

The next day, though, we had to go through the same exchange. It was no longer a courtroom examination but a catechism, and I was not happy about it, having better things to do with my time and energy than confess to this young pup how I envied him and how he was fortune's darling, more richly rewarded than he deserved to be. I decided, in fact, to cut the tiresome business short by requesting leave, to which I was entitled anyway. I thought that a trip home to Vienna would do me good. The chances were better than even that Stefan would meanwhile find someone else to appeal to, another old rake to whom he could turn for endorsement or validation or approval. It was up to him to decide whether he wanted to grow up and live for himself, relying upon his own feelings and trusting his own heart and mind. I told him that was what he would have to do, sooner or later, but I knew, even as my words formed in my mouth, that I might as well have been addressing his horse.

My leave granted, I set out for Vienna, where I planned to spend a relaxed and amusing fortnight. The visit began well enough, but toward the end of the first week, I sprained my ankle. It was one of those silly accidents, but because I had been engaged in an attempt—successful, I'm glad to say—to save the life of a pretty woman's poodle that had bolted after a cat and was about to be run down by a large barouche, my trivial mishap brought me not only an introduction to the woman but the notice of General von D——, whose protégée she turned out to be. I hadn't known of her connection to the general, having been out of town with the regiment, but that didn't make any difference. I'd have tried to save the little dog's life either way, and in neither case would it have been particularly noble on my part. Lust or careerism, what's the difference?

But I was successful, handed her the small dog, and then, realizing for the first time that there was something wrong with my left ankle, nearly collapsed in the street.

I was taken to a military hospital, examined, and told I'd need to stay off the foot for at least a week. I made no objection to this. I was pleasantly surprised when the woman whose dog I'd rescued showed up the next day to be sure I was comfortable and to supply me with a hamper of delicacies and a package of books. That was in the morning. In the afternoon, the general himself came through to pay me a visit and thank me. Was there anything he could do to make my stay more agreeable?

"You are most kind, general. As you see, I am admirably well fixed here. I am delighted to have been able to be of service to the charming young lady, and to you, and to have saved her little dog. This is as comfortable a way of spending my leave as anything I can imagine," I told him. I wasn't hinting about an extension of my leave. I meant it, sincerely. I had a private room with a view of a pleasant park. I had books. I had a hamper of goodies. As long as I stayed off my ankle, I was quite comfortable.

The general, however, insisted that I should not forfeit any of my amusements or diversions on account of an act of chivalry in the best tradition of military service. He would order my leave extended.

"The general is most gracious," I told him.

"The captain is most gallant," he replied. "I shall be proud to speak of your brave deed to General Leinsdorf himself."

"I expected no credit for a small service to a beautiful woman," I said.

He gave me a long slow wink, which was a peculiar signal for a general to offer a captain. It was intimate and suggested either that I was a chip off General Leinsdorf's old block, or that he appreciated my compliment to his taste in women, or that he regretted I had exerted myself to impress a woman who was spoken for. All of those, perhaps. We are all men of the world, together, eh?

I thought of Stefan, whose need for such reassurance I had attributed to his youth and inexperience. Before me, however, was a man in his late fifties or early sixties, his chest covered with decorations, his head barely able to support the grand hat he wore with its badges of office, and he was inviting the same kind of approval. We all do it, every man jack of us. I promised myself I'd be more tolerant of Stefan when I returned, or that I'd make an effort.

I was away almost two months, my leave having been extravagantly extended and my presence having then been required in Vienna for a court-martial that was supposed to take three days and took almost two weeks. We met every morning at ten, listened to witnesses until noon, broke for lunch until two-thirty, listened to more testimony until four, and then had our evenings free. An agreeable life, and almost certainly a further evidence of General Von D——'s appreciation, but it came to an end and I prepared to resume my not very onerous duties back with the regiment at Waldenburg. Nothing had changed. Nothing ever does. The only difference was that Stefan was no longer hanging about, eager to discuss with me every variation in his mood or every emotional tremor in the Krasinska ménage. He had found another officer in whom to confide, I assumed, and I was not displeased to have been relieved of that burden.

But, no, there was something more to it. I could tell from Stefan's military bearing, from the wooden drill-field quality of his movements and expression that he was troubled, had taken what we call internal leave. He was, I discovered, actually avoiding me—which I should have appreciated only a couple of months before but which now worried me. What new disaster had befallen him, or all three of them together?

I considered the obvious and even banal possibility, but dismissed it. Peasant girls, ignorant and careless, might get pregnant. Scheming shopgirls from the city, desperate enough to gamble everything, might risk it. But an intelligent girl like Eugenie, brought up among women like her mother and Wanda? It was possible, of course. It could happen to anyone, no matter what sensible precautions she took or how scrupulously she observed the rules of the game.

There had to be another explanation for his gloom, something more serious. Or less serious that affected him at a sensitive point. I waited a few days, thinking to let him come to me, but when he didn't, I went to him. I was interested, had allowed myself to be drawn into this business, had promised myself back in Vienna to be more charitable and understanding. "What's the trouble? You look as though you'd been assigned to a firing squad."

"I wish I had been," Stefan told me. "As the target."

"Nothing could be that bad."

"Eugenie's pregnant."

I hardly hesitated. "Congratulations!" I said. I seized his hand and pumped it warmly. "What wonderful news!"

135

XXVII · *A Lure*

The lieutenant was less than delighted with himself and he was all the more uncomfortable because a part of him was honestly attracted to the idea of marriage, which was now the subject of all their conversations, obfuscations, and silences. It loomed over them like a cloud, or under them like the name of a painting, marking the frame of their lives. *The Lieutenant Considers Matrimony.*

The girl was intelligent, pretty, original, and fond of him. The house was comfortable. The mother was no mean asset, herself.

"What's the problem, then?" I asked him. "You seem to lack a certain enthusiasm."

"I feel trapped," he told me.

"You think they planned to trap you? You think it was a deliberate thing?"

"No. In fact, Eugenie isn't absolutely sure she wants to marry me. She would, I'm sure, if I asked her. Her mother would talk her into it. But it would be a kind of defeat for her. It would mean having to give up all her ideas of freedom and independence."

"And you don't want her to give them up? Or don't want to give them up, yourself?"

"I never much believed in them. But I think she did, and I can't suppose that she would have set out to get pregnant in order to force a marriage. I'm sure she wouldn't have done that."

"But you still feel trapped."

"Yes. And Sonja knows that."

"She's the one who's pressing you?"

"She's a realist. She knows the baby needs a father. And she knows I'm a 'man of honor' and 'will do the right thing.'"

"Well? Won't you?"

"I suppose I must. But I feel trapped, nevertheless. I feel that it's out of control."

"But that's not their fault, is it? That has more to do with time. If you were on the battlefield and you were so badly wounded that you knew you'd no chance to survive and could feel your life pouring out, there would be that same sensation, wouldn't there? That something had happened in the past that was dictating the future about which you had no say any more—that's what you can't stand. But our lives are like that. It's hard, but there it is."

"I have the feeling it's a terrible mistake."

"Yes, but it's your mistake. You can take a kind of pride in that. It's a destiny you've found for yourself. You're not out there on a battlefield of indiscriminate carnage where the same destiny has included hundreds and thousands of others. This is your own particular mess. There's honor in that, I've always thought."

He was disappointingly unresponsive. I had fashioned a conceit that had in it some philosophical truth, a deep and trustworthy resonance, but he refused to take courage or comfort or even pleasure in what I'd been able to serve up, impromptu, to meet his dreary occasion.

Never for a moment did I wonder if he was considering whether to tell me the rest of it. I'd heard enough to make my *mot*, and didn't require a rest. But there was more. There often is.

Only later on was I able to gather in the essential bit of information he was aching to impart to me, sick with it but unable to cough it up and spit it out. The girl was not the problem, or no more of a problem than she had been from the first moment their paths had crossed. It was Sonja who had terrified Stefan, pushing him harder than she should have, forgetting herself and her characteristic shrewdness out of a perfectly reasonable concern for her child, her poor lame duckling, whom she wanted to protect and for whom she was all too willing to sacrifice. In a scene I have often imagined, she confronted him to ask him, yet again, what he wanted to do.

"Marry, I suppose," he told her. But his look would have been downcast, resigned, as if some other possible outcome might be hidden in the luster of his boots' polished toes.

"Not the likeliest chance of happiness, is it?" she asked.

He looked up at her, startled. She was supposed to be arguing on the other side, after all.

"Your reluctance shows. If to me, then to Eugenie as well. And to the rest of the world, in time. It's not an auspicious beginning to a matrimonial adventure."

"It's not so unusual," he said. "Certainly, it's not without precedent. And some of those marriages, I'm sure, have worked out well enough."

"But she is a superb girl, an extraordinary girl. As you are an extraordinary young man. You deserve the very best, both of you. Each and both."

"You don't think we should marry?"

"I think you should want to. You should be eager to. And only in that event should you marry. Neither of you should have to settle for the other."

"It's not that. I'm not settling for her. I think she is, as you say, extraordinary. But she's young. And I'm very young. I've just begun my career. It's not what I'd planned."

"That doesn't make it altogether a tragedy, though, does it? You have stumbled upon a great treasure. Is it worth any the less because you had not set out to hunt for such a treasure?"

"No, of course not."

"I cannot advise you. But she will not consider a match she thinks is being forced upon her. Or that she suspects you are forced into, even by your own sense of honor."

"Yes, I can see that. She wouldn't."

"But if you were enthusiastic, really excited about the idea, then she might allow herself to be persuaded, even in spite of George Sand."

"Yes, she would, wouldn't she."

"I wonder, then, what it would require for you to feel that excitement and to express, quite sincerely, that enthusiasm. I've been thinking of the curious way we began, the three of us, and wondering whether that wasn't what you'd wanted all along. For you and Eugenie to marry wouldn't prevent us from returning to that earlier arrangement. It would depend, I think, on what you wanted and what she wanted. I'm happy to see the two of you happy, if you take my meaning, and would be delighted to do all in my power, whatever is necessary . . ."

"Yes, yes, I see," he said. And probably added something suitably polite, not knowing what else to say but unable to leave it unadorned and stark: "You are most kind" or "It's a lovely idea."

In fact, he was rather frightened by it. The game was the same as what they'd been playing earlier, but the stakes were higher now. A marriage. A child. An official series of rites and documents, beginning with the permission of the commander and continuing endlessly, beyond any horizon he could imagine. He realized, in other words, that he was playing with nothing less than his life—which is a truth the women had of course understood from the beginning and had long ago managed to accept.

If he had any complaint about them, it might properly have been that their bravery was deceptive and had misled him. He was the one in the gaudy uniform with the shako and epaulets, but they were the virtuosas of daring. He had relied on their ordinariness, their domesticity, the absence of jingling spurs and flashing sabers, forgetting that the salute is an appropriate greeting from an officer to a woman, originated with such a confrontation, and was only extended, later, to include fellow soldiers.

He was also intimidated by the unconventionality of the

mother's suggestion. To spend a month or two in such a ménage had seemed a kind of naughty fun, but there had never been any necessity to admit it was real, that it was he, that it was anything other than an improbable lark. He just didn't have the nerve to think of what he'd already done except as a lapse from another reality, another standard, imprecise perhaps but undemanding—the way most people seem to live.

It was with her offer in mind that he'd come to talk to me, and I didn't listen hard or patiently enough. It was his fault as much as mine. He might have chosen his moment better, or persisted longer, or tried again. But he didn't. And having tried and failed to raise the subject with me, he was now worse off than ever, for he had reached, for the first time in his life, an understanding of the word we bandy about but seldom mean literally: He had ventured into a realm of behavior, a way of life, that was "unspeakable."

He felt himself to be a monster, and in his awful isolation it seemed to him that in either case, accepting her proposal or rejecting it, he would be behaving in a monstrous way.

XXVIII · *The Dream Come True*

Whatever Stefan's private torments, there could not be any other outcome than that with greater or less resignation he should at last face the colonel of the regiment and, in proper military style, request permission for marriage.

Colonel Bergner would have been avuncular, in conformity with his idea of himself as universally beloved and admired, an illusion none of us wanted to shatter for fear of letting our commander's real nature show itself more plainly than it already did. Because he thought of himself as a dear old fellow, he moderated, to some extent, his natural inclination to be a martinet. He would almost certainly have come around to lean on the front of his desk—informal, man to man, and cozy, or a cartoon of those qualities—to advise young Stefan that he was, well, er, ah, rather . . . young.

"I appreciate that, sir," Stefan must have replied.

"As one grows older, one may not grow any wiser, but one comes to know oneself better. One settles into life a little more securely . . ." Et cetera. One can go on in the impersonal third person, sounding lofty and knowing, for soporific hours, particularly if one is Colonel Bergner. My own trick is to look at the tip of his nose, so that I appear to be wholly attentive and eager for each new word, each fresh-minted syllable.

Stefan endured these philosophical maunderings about youth and self-knowledge. Then, when they had subsided, he spoke up, agreeing with the colonel, appreciating his concern, and endorsing the wisdom of his remarks. "The fact remains, sir, that I do not have the freedom to follow the valuable advice you've offered me. I must have permission to marry. Or I must resign my commission."

At that point, the informality was at an end. The colonel got up, walked back to his chair behind the desk, seated himself, and stared balefully across the expanse of polished wood, fiddling with a letter opener as if it were a dagger. "And if I were to give my permission for a wedding that was to take place a year from now?"

"I'd have to resign my commission," Stefan said.

"I see."

A long pause. Or, more than that, a stretch of silence during which the colonel struggled with himself, his severe impulses wrestling with his fantasies about what a wonderful fellow he was, a cuddly bear, a comrade in arms, an older brother, a wise pal. And not at all incidentally, Stefan had to wait it out, worrying, knowing that his destiny hung on the colonel's whim.

The colonel delighted in his display of power. What a luxury, to be able to decide what kind of man to be and what destinies therefore will arise from this deliberated self that will affect the rest of the regiment, the rest of the world. How marvelously exhilarating! And yet, if the colonel had given an honest and spontaneous answer, either yes or no, he might have averted the disaster. It was his posturing that caused—as much as anything can be said to have caused—the debacle.

Finally, having satisfied himself that the last drop of juice had been squeezed from the moment's flesh, he allowed Stefan a watery smile—of indulgent disappointment? *Weltschmerz? Schadenfreude?*—and a soft sigh. "Well, in that event, I suppose I must grant your request. And I offer my congratulations to the lieutenant and his fiancée."

"I am most grateful," Stefan said, his eyes burning.

The colonel put the letter opener down, centered on the desk, its point toward Stefan. It was as if a court-martial had found him guilty and the sword had been arranged on the table with its blade toward the defendant.

Stefan stood at attention. The colonel dismissed him. He walked out to the parade ground, emerging into the brightness like a nocturnal animal driven from its lair into the unfamiliar and dangerous glare of midday. The colonel knew! His wife was a trollop and a whore, and he was a whoremaster! There would be sniggers and coarse jokes throughout the regiment. Somehow the rest of it would come out, the depravity of the mother, the incredible voluptuary tendencies he had discovered in himself, the unimaginable depravity . . .

Some such dreadful thoughts must have hounded him. He felt himself to be utterly ruined, and a fool as well. If he had been less polite to the colonel, less of a bootlicker, more loyal to Eugenie and Sonja, then the colonel might have accepted the resignation of his commission. That would have been a way out. He stopped, considered turning back, imagined himself marching into the colonel's office and announcing, "With the colonel's permission, sir, the lieutenant wishes to observe that the colonel is a pompous ass. And a knave. And that the colonel eats shit, sir. And that the colonel's mother eats shit!"

But he knew he'd never be able to get the words out, that his voice would desert him.

Anyway, it wouldn't work. Instead of accepting Stefan's resignation, the colonel would send him off to a military prison or, more probably, a madhouse. Meanwhile, Eugenie's belly would continue to grow, his destiny ballooning out and looming over him like a cloud that blotted out the sky.

The following Sunday at our weekly feast, the colonel announced the engagement. Stefan seemed nervous, a bit self-conscious, but generally pleased. And for his part, I must say that the colonel performed creditably, his artificial heartiness exactly what it would have been had there not been a necessity to the marriage. I was a little surprised, though, by the details of the announcement. The wedding would be held here, at the barracks, in formal uniform. The very thing Stefan had seized upon back at the beginning as an emblem of all his worries. I could see it at once, the arch of crossed swords under which the bride and groom would march together. Could she perhaps, leaning on his rigid arm, walk without that rolling gait, drawing strength from him, so that, for one instant in her life, she could be excused from her imperfection, be the ideal bride any girl deserves to imagine herself?

After the meal, I offered my congratulations, leaving it to Stefan to decide whether he wanted to confide in me, connecting what I knew of the past to what he had recently determined about the future. He chose not to say anything, but he did invite me to be his best man, standing up with him.

"I'd be honored," I told him. I supposed it might be his way of expunging the past.

"The colonel will be giving the bride away, marching down the aisle with her," he told me, "her father having died."

"Wonderful," I said.

Was he crazy? Was it some satirical gesture? Or was it bitterness? Then, again, it might be a strict observance of the norms of military etiquette that had no significance of any kind. Could I believe that?

No, not really. Not for a minute.

XXIX · *Maneuver*

I imagined another more cheerful Stefan bringing home the news of Colonel Bergner's permission to an anxious Eugenie and taking some pleasure in her show of pleasure. The joys of youth are secondary joys, reflecting the moods of others. Not knowing their own minds, the young take what cues they can from the world around them and feel happy or sad just as chameleons show themselves brown or green, harmonizing with whatever tint and mood they happen upon. Eugenie ought to have been relieved by the colonel's decision, but she would have expressed this feeling as delight, either out of shrewdness or from simple feminine tact.

Or am I being too fanciful? There is a simpler, more accurate way of describing the peculiar accommodations these youngsters kept making and then repairing. They were enchanted with each other, but the spells were those of novice magicians and never lasted very long. It is not so difficult to turn the frog into a prince, but to keep him there, maintaining his princeliness despite his wandering attention—and that of the enchantress too—that is the great challenge.

What happened, then, was a series of mutual spells, incantations, rituals, and enchantments, never enduring, never quite coordinated, not to be taken too seriously, but not to be too quickly dismissed either. The proposal, for example, was a detail Stefan had simply neglected, having assumed that the mother had spoken on behalf of her daughter and that the agreement of the one included and bound the other. The rationale was clear, for the mother had subordinated her interests to those of her daughter. Was it not reasonable to suppose that Eugenie would be willing to accept the hand of the lieutenant, having already accepted other parts of him, not only for herself but for the sake of their unborn child as well? Was it likely that she would ruin her own prospects merely to assert her independence of spirit and deny that she was a creature either of her mother or of interest itself?

That, of course, is exactly what she did. The lieutenant, in whatever mood of leaden stoicism, returned to the Krasinska houshold to tell Eugenie about Colonel Bergner's permission to marry, and she startled him by asking, "And what about my own permission?"

"I thought you had agreed . . ."

"When? I remember no such agreement. A proposal of marriage is not likely to have slipped my mind."

It was clearly a joke. At the worst, she wanted him to conform to the ritual, to say the prescribed words in the prescribed way. Getting down on one knee, then, he asked her, "Eugenie, will you do me the honor of becoming my wife?"

"Certainly not."

"No?"

"No!"

He managed not to laugh, even though she was being perfectly ridiculous and despite the fact that he could imagine himself back at the barracks trying to explain this to the colonel, who naturally would be more concerned with Stefan's having made him look awkward than with any discomfort the foolish lieutenant might be experiencing.

"You won't marry me, even for the child's sake?"

"No, I won't. It's not free. It goes against everything I believe in," she said. "For your sake and for mine, I can't marry you."

"That's very fine," Stefan told her. "It sounds wonderful and lofty and noble, but it's stupid. You know that, don't you?"

"I'm not surprised that you think so."

"And your mother? What does she think?"

146

"I am sure she agrees with you," Eugenie admitted. "She wants me to be practical."

"So do I."

"*Impractical* and *stupid* are not necessarily the same," she declared grandly.

"Who do you think you are?" he asked. "A countess? A duchess? For most of the world, there is no difference at all. Practical means intelligent. Impractical is stupid."

"Naturally, you believe that."

He had no idea how to deal with her or what there was behind her infuriating superiority. I had never told him the family secret, which caused Eugenie both pride and shame, of her paternity. He had come close, asking whether she thought she was a countess or a duchess. In fact, her conviction that princely blood flowed in her veins, and therefore in the baby's too, made her think herself immune from all the vulgar concerns of ordinary people. If she were to give in to them and obey the commands of common sense, she would be abandoning her birthright. She had to be more scrupulous than if she had been a legitimate Radziwill because she had nothing to fall back on for confirmation and support. Her sense of herself was all she had in the way of palaces, lands, decorations, and letters patent.

Stefan thought she was merely crazy. "In that case," he said, "I'll marry your mother."

"Fine," she said. "Do that. I'm sure the two of you will be happy together."

It had been a desperate remark, spoken in anger and without thought. But he supposed there was something to be said for the idea. He could go through with a wedding, which might satisfy the colonel. He and Sonja could even adopt the child, which would then bear his name . . .

But it was no good. What was he thinking? She could not possibly want him to marry her mother. He didn't want to do that. Why was she making everything so difficult, and in the name of spontaneity and freedom? "Why must you make life so difficult?" he asked.

147

"If I give in now," she answered, "it will only be more difficult later. One must take a stand sooner or later, and it is always more difficult later."

"Do you really want me to marry your mother?" he asked. "Is that what you want to do?"

"I promised her I'd marry you. I asked the colonel's permission to marry. I'm committed already . . ."

"That's exactly what I mean," she said, but it wasn't triumph in her voice. Gentle regret was what he heard. "It is a commitment. It isn't free any more, is it?"

"It would have been."

"You are sweet to say so," she told him. "We can still be friends, though."

It was the conventional remark, but there was something in her tone that was not at all conventional and spoke not of friendship but love. Teasingly, annoyingly, she was letting him know that he would still be welcome in her bed. He thought her the most unreasonable, willful, arbitrary woman who had ever lived.

"I'm glad to hear it," he said. He considered telling her about her mother's offer, but he couldn't quite bring himself to do that. Instead, he realized that the way to reach her was on the high road of abstraction and theory. "You know," he said, "there might be a way out for us after all, a way to maintain that freedom you prize so much."

"Oh?"

He was encouraged by her willingness to listen, her friendliness, and even, if he was not altogether deluding himself, her hopefulness. "We could agree, between us, that the ceremony was entirely for the benefit of the child. We could, in effect, exempt ourselves from it, understanding that it was a *mariage de convenance* . . ."

". . . with no ties of any kind," she chimed in, making no effort at all to hide her enthusiasm.

"Exactly. Your mother would be relieved. The baby would be provided for. And yet, you and I would retain our independence of spirit."

Those were all good reasons, but what he had blundered into was an appeal to her aristocratic pretensions. It is princesses and duchesses who contract for such marriages, not seamstresses and flower girls. He had acknowledged her rank without actually referring to it (she was touchy about it, I expect, and interpreted any overt reference as possibly sarcastic, a challenge as much as an acknowledgment). He thought, however, that he had taken the properly abstract high ground, had conceived a plan, maneuvered correctly, and had executed it precisely. There was a mordant satisfaction he was able to take in what he thought he'd done, and he was pleased to allow her to lead him upstairs to her bed.

XXX · Jeu de Cartes

The regimental silver had never looked more impressive—or more oppressive with its intimidating weight and vain opulence. I kept thinking that these table decorations were the gifts and legacies of brother officers, men who had died without issue, younger sons, most of them, who had detested their families and named the regiment as their heir, specifying the silver collection because of its enduring ghastliness. The gesture was rather like that of the monks of certain orders who leave their bones to be used for the macabre decorations of their chapter's ossuary, a bequest peculiarly constituted of love and hatred in almost equal measure. Our silver, ornately worked with its garlands of flowers and wreaths of leaves and vines, approached the same high pitch of horribilitude—at least to my eye and taste that evening. Of all the monuments to leave behind, our dreadful stirrup cups or our elaborate candelabra came as close to the nihilist ideal as anything I had ever seen.

My admittedly glum musings occupied me during the course of the dinner party, as did the silver surfaces that distorted the reflections of the officers and the colonel and his wife, our gracious hosts that evening. Next to them were our guests of honor, Eugenie Krasinska and her mother, beside whom the young lieutenant sat smiling out at us in a somewhat glassy bonhomie.

I attributed his soddenness to a quite understandable self-consciousness. He was not used to being the center of attention. He was venturing forth into unknown territory. He was a bit young for matrimony, after all. But he was not too young to be shot at. And if the worst came to pass and he decided to resign his commission and throw his lot in with the Krasinskas, all he was really sacrificing was some childish dream of military glory in which he was too intelligent to believe anyway. He would have his child, a whole brood of them no doubt, and pursue some sensible career in commerce, perhaps embellishing himself with a minor official function, as notary or even magistrate, the kind of thing that entitles one, after many years, to a small rosette in the buttonhole and respectful titles on envelopes and invitations.

It was a comedown, perhaps, for Eugenie, a sacrifice of interesting pretensions—interesting to me, at any rate. But Stefan had no way of knowing this. He was wrapped up in his own situation, his own drama, and he listened to the conventional toasts and speeches wishing him and his bride all good things as if he were scrutinizing each of them for overt sarcasm or impertinence. There was something fierce in his bland grin, or so I thought then, but I dismissed it because I couldn't make sense of it. I was right to see it, wrong to trust my intellect too far and reject what I could not understand.

That ugly silver prompted me to think he'd be well off if he were to get out and lead a normal life, surrounded by objects designed to be used by normal people in reasonable domestic ways. A draught of cold water from a crockery pitcher tastes just as good as one from the great chased ewer with nymphs supporting the lip of its spout, particularly if one remembers Captain Dretsen of the ready laugh and reliable friendliness, in whose memory the vessel is supposed to stand. As easily as cold water, blood might come pouring forth from that spout, cold enough now to account for the matte finish condensation gives sterling.

"Long life! Long life!" we all bellowed, the conventional reply to yet another conventional toast. My impression was that most of the officers were feeling more or less the way I did, that she was a pretty girl, that Stefan had been perhaps a bit precipitant, falling in love with the daughter in the very

151

first household in which he'd been billeted, but the consensus was that she was not a bad match. I certainly heard nothing against her—and no one was so crude as to make any reference to an all but imperceptible deformity. These were gentlemen, after all, even if they were young and, in some instances, a bit callow. For that matter, I think it was Stefan's own callowness, his recognition of the temptation in himself to make such jokes at other people's expense, that had put the peculiar fear into his soul in the first place.

Colonel Bergner was charmed by Sonja and her daughter and felt himself vindicated—for he had stretched a point or two, risking what he conceived to be the honor of the regiment, and there was no cause for worry. The Krasinskas would be altogether acceptable. He had two criteria, both curious, but they were at least explicit. He asked himself how the future wives of his officers would grace a dinner table—meaning his own, of course. And Eugenie was properly deferential and admiring without being altogether dull. And then, he asked himself how they would look and comport themselves dressed in widow's weeds, accepting the flag that had draped their fallen husband's caskets. Presumably she was suitably touching in this mental cartoon of his. He became almost convivial by the end of the evening.

He gave Stefan the honor of proposing the last toast of the night—to the regiment!—rounding off the long series that had begun with the first, to the emperor. We drained our glasses. The colonel made it clear how pleased he was with Eugenie by sending the Krasinskas home in his own carriage. Stefan remained, of course, for cigars and port, and a few hands of cards.

In the unbuttoned atmosphere of the cardroom, there were more informal congratulations, cheerful and comradely, which Stefan accepted quietly and without suspicion. It was only the unfortunate locution of Lieutenant Kremsier that produced, out of a clear sky, the ominous flash of summer lightning and the crash of thunder. "Wonderfully fast work, old sport," Kremsier said, adding for reasons no one will ever know, "you must have swept her right off her feet."

Stefan went quite white. He rose to attention, clenched his fists, so that I thought he well might strike Kremsier, but restrained himself and instead said, sotto voce and choked with anger, "I demand an immediate apology, sir."

"I apologize," Kremsier said, cheerfully obliging. "I never meant . . ."

"You need say no more. The matter is closed. I accept your apology," Stefan said. He turned away and walked from the room.

"It never even crossed my mind," Kremsier announced to the rest of us. "I'd forgotten entirely there was anything wrong with her foot."

"Drop it," I suggested.

"I really didn't mean to hurt his feelings," he said.

"I'm sure. But let it go."

I went to the sideboard for a brandy, feeling the risk of the moment only now that it was past. Young enough and certainly foolish enough, Stefan might have manipulated Kremsier and himself into an entanglement from which there was but one way out. He'd been unstable enough, so that I could imagine him wanting to end up on the field of honor, having his brains blown out before breakfast.

My temptation was to go out onto the veranda where I knew he'd be standing, posing in the moonlight, cultivating whatever humors and fantasies the cry of the owls might suggest to him, and I actually started in that direction, but my second thought was to let him cool off a bit. He'd handled himself well, all things considered. He'd accepted Kremsier's apology at any rate, and for all I knew, he might be standing there, smoking a cigar and waiting for his pulse to return to something close to normal. For me to intrude on that would be to betray my fears about his ability to dismiss an unfortunate remark and would be, in its way, a fresh insult.

He did return to the cardroom after perhaps a quarter of an hour and invited me to play a few hands of cards with him.

"Why not?" I asked, delighted that he was demonstrating—to me in particular—his equanimity. "I'd be only too pleased."

"Splendid," he said, perhaps too brightly. "And to make it interesting, a mark or two?"

"If you like," I agreed.

We began to play bezique and the talers and schillings and marks and golden zlotys started to pile up. He played recklessly, and I thought many times of trying to dissuáde him, but what could I have said that would have been at all effective and not offensive? I thought he might be sowing wild oats, being aggressively irresponsible before settling down for his lifetime of prudence and reasonableness and domestic comfort. I thought he might be defying the gods in some way, demanding of them a small fortune as his due because, having been unlucky at love (forced, at any rate, to marry), he was supposed to be lucky at cards. It crossed my mind that he might be trying to win, to recoup initial losses that he couldn't afford and set himself up either for a wedding trip or some business enterprise. He had not picked an appropriate opponent, however, for if I had the Hapsburg jaw, I did not have the Hapsburg fortune to go with it. And I had more skill than he, so that his recklessness was, at least in the beginning, an opportunity for me. It occurred to me to try to lose, but I could not risk his guessing what I was doing. In any case, if he was fated to lose—or determined to lose—better to me than to another, richer officer. He ran out of pocket money quickly enough and began writing IOUs, which I could not refuse.

"Perhaps we ought to call a halt after one more hand?" I suggested. "It's getting late after all."

"I must win back," he said. "I cannot let it go like this."

"If you insist," I told him, but my apprehension was growing by the moment. There was no realistic hope at all of his winning back the considerable sum he'd already lost. What was obvious to me—and might be dimly perceptible to Stefan—was that he was going to lose more. It even occurred to me that he'd chosen me deliberately as the man to whom he wanted to lose, but I could not account for this. I remembered the confession of an old friend of my mother's, an in-

154

veterate gambler, who told me that the sensation of winning was small, certainly pleasant but minor, the equivalent of choosing a bonbon from a box and finding one has avoided the almond center one dislikes and has hit upon a caramel of which one is particularly fond. On the other hand, the sensation of losing was unpleasant but huge, all-encompassing, major, like taking a jump in skiing and feeling the earth fall away below. The real gambler lives for that moment, feels alive only at such critical instants.

It was possible that Stefan had decided, in this final evening of his bachelorhood, to feel himself at risk, to enjoy the desperation and peculiar liveliness that come with losing an impressive sum. He had picked me because I would not hound him, might even forgive the debt. He'd picked me as a way of hedging his bet a little. Certainly, that was what I hoped, and it seemed reasonable because I knew I'd be prepared in a moment to forgive his debt and tear up his chits, and not only prepared but relieved to do so. As a wedding gift, perhaps? A friendly gesture like that could not offend even the most sensitive young officer, could it?

I actually think I asked myself that question. I remember answering it with less certainty than felt comfortable and trying to find other ways in which I might solve the problem that was growing in seriousness with each hand. I could cheat, actually contrive to lose. And I did play recklessly, hoping in that way to restore some of his losses, but there were limits beyond which I dared not go lest he think I was trying to lose. It never even crossed my mind that he, too, might be trying to lose.

At one point, quite late in the evening—or night, really— he asked, "Where are we now?"

"You don't want to know," I told him.

"I insist," he said and he reached across the table to snatch up his chits. He counted them, mumbling to himself as he did the sums in his head. "Forty-seven thousand!"

"Surely it can't be that much. You must have made a mistake," I said, reaching for them. "Let me count them."

He was alert to what I might try to do. He counted them again, aloud, putting them down, one by one, on the green baize in front of him. It was that extravagant precision people sometimes affect when they have had too much to drink. His arithmetic was accurate, however. It did, indeed, come to forty-seven thousand.

"Double or nothing?" I offered, resolved now to lose, determined not to be outmaneuvered.

"Done," he agreed. "I'll deal."

There is though, an element of luck in the game. One can do everything right and lose. One can also do everything wrong and win, if one's partner is also behaving in a willfully foolish manner. I tried as hard as I could to discard any card that looked attractive, but there were always new cards with the potential for victory hidden under the elaborate arabesques of their blue and white backs.

"Congratulations," he said at the end of the hand. "It is now ninety-four thousand. You're a rich man!"

"We'll talk about it tomorrow," I said as gently as I could.

"Certainly, tomorrow. By all means, tomorrow. 'Une dette de jeu, une dette d'honneur, vingt-quatre heures.'"

He lurched out to Sonja Krasinska's carriage to go home, leaving me sitting there, my chin resting in the palm of my hand, appalled by what I had allowed to happen. "Fool!" I muttered under my breath, not at all sure whether I meant Stefan or myself.

XXXI · *Rite of Passage*

The wedding was hardly a proper occasion for me to raise so awkward a subject as Stefan's gambling debt, even to try to forgive it. His aunt and uncle had journeyed from Vienna to attend the ceremony, but the aunt had not felt up to the prenuptial party, so neither of them had appeared at the colonel's dinner. She may in fact have been stricken with the headache she claimed. It was clear, however, that neither of them felt enthusiasm for the match. On the morning of the wedding, her expression and carriage all but shouted the disdain it would have been redundant for her to express in words.

It is also possible that I am exaggerating. Not inconceivably, that was her permanent expression, her constant response to a world that seemed to her a continual affront. Her husband, meanwhile, looked to be quietly enduring—the world, his nephew, his wife, his life. That almost stagey deference Stefan showed them both was in good measure sarcastic, a mode of behavior I expect he had probably devised as a youngster and the three of them found mutually acceptable. I could certainly understand Stefan's need to be rid of such people, clinging to the regiment and its traditions as a better connection than the one he had enjoyed—or hadn't—with the two of them.

His relatives and I had little to say to one another, even though I did make an effort, in my capacity as best man. I tried to engage them in small talk and thereby protect Stefan from their attentions. It was hard going, however, and their grudging dispensation of monosyllables led me at last to sup-

157

pose I might make myself more useful in the performance of other, more agreeable duties. I returned to Stefan, who appeared to have been supplied with a fairly convincing wooden mask of his features.

"Nervous?" I asked him.

"Not at all."

"It's perfectly acceptable to be nervous. It's even expected, I'd say."

"Is it?"

"So I'm told."

"I can't think why."

"It's one of those big moments," I told him. "One's whole life is hanging in the balance. One has the feeling of having made a momentous decision." My tone was cheerful, even congratulatory. I wasn't trying to frighten him but only to get him to relax a little, to enjoy the moment, or at least experience some of it and come out of what was very close to a trance.

He made no answer at all. I might as well have been speaking in some language with which he was unfamiliar. He simply turned away.

I opened the vestry door a crack and peered into the church. It was a small village church that had been decked with flowers and hung about with our regimental standards and pennons, so the effect was rather that of a shrunken cathedral. The last stragglers were being seated. The priest, a youngster not much older than Stefan, was considering his remarks or perhaps praying for guidance. This parish, I think, was his first posting. I had the impression that he wanted very much for the ceremony to go smoothly as if it were a drill-field exercise. The great number of dress uniforms must have dazzled him or led him to believe that we in the regiment expected precision and would judge him on his ability to achieve it. He might also have had stage fright.

He cleared his throat several times, looked down at the floor, up to the ceiling, and seeing no other way out, asked us if we were ready to begin. I looked to Stefan. He nodded and then I nodded.

"Let us take our places then."

We followed the priest out of the vestry and crossed the small transept to take our places before the altar. We knelt, crossed ourselves, and rose. The priest nodded to an elderly gentleman in the choir loft who began to play the harmonium, which was the signal for the bride to appear from the far end of the nave. I watched her, dressed in white and carrying a nosegay. Walking beside her, his left arm extended to offer her support, Colonel Bergner seemed at least as radiant as Eugenie, his sword hanging from its scarlet sash, his medals making an impressive display on both sides of his chest, and his cockaded tricorn cradled in his right arm as if it were an imperial crown.

I had heard, in those many wearisome sessions of self-analysis, doubt, and resolution, an expression of Stefan's persistent fears of how Eugenie would look one day if they ever reached the point of getting married. He was worried—as every man is, I suppose—what his fellow officers would think of his bride and whether they would find her acceptable. Would they approve of her and therefore of his choice, or would they feel pity or even laugh? He had imagined her lurching crazily down the aisle like a cart about to lose one of its wheels or a top that has run down and is now making a series of helpless twirls and dips, careening to the deathly stillness that already seems physically to weigh upon it. It wasn't nearly so bad as he'd feared, but still, standing there beside him and having heard him voice his apprehensions about how she would look at this particular moment, I was aware that she did roll just a little. I was more acutely sensible of it than was anyone else in the church—except Stefan, of course, and perhaps Sonja, and Eugenie herself. But I was relieved at how slight was the variation from the normal or, as Stefan would have put it, the perfect. It was a mere detail, insignificant if he loved her and not at all important if he didn't. Why, then, his too soldierly impassivity, his excessively military bearing in which I thought I detected the same sarcasm as had always characterized his deference to his aunt and uncle? He was just nervous, I kept telling myself, and too much aware of the histrionic demands of the occasion.

With some delicacy and rather more meaning than the gesture usually carries, Colonel Bergner handed Eugenie to Stefan, giving over to the groom his role as the girl's support. The young priest then commenced the wedding service, reading it through in proper form and even, at the appropriate moment, stopping to offer his good wishes and prayers as much as his advice. It was, indeed, his first wedding and he took, he said, a special pride and concern for its longevity and happiness. He hoped the good Lord would watch over the union with the fondness that he, the Lord's servant, felt and prayed for.

He returned to the book and completed the service. Stefan turned to me and I produced the ring he placed on Eugenie's finger. The priest pronounced them man and wife. Stefan kissed the bride and then led her back down the aisle, feeling whatever pride or horror or numb satisfaction he was able to derive from this accurate enactment of his nightmare, for, indeed, just as he had always known, there was a detail waiting outside for them in dress uniform, their drawn swords forming a series of arches, a kind of canopy under which he was to lead his wife to their carriage. In his effort to get her down the steps, through those half-dozen arches of gleaming steel, and into the waiting carriage, he was more hurried than he should have been, and it was his fault that she stumbled slightly. She recovered almost immediately and even managed to smile at him to let him know that she was all right, that everything would be all right, and that she was happy, but he looked ashen, furious with her or, more likely, with himself.

Had it been just an unfortunate moment and not so weighted, so posed, with the entire regiment assembled on the lawn of the church on the steps of which those twelve men stood with their swords still presented in salute, I would have called out. I was even tempted to run after them, fling myself into the seat beside them, and tell him he was wrong, that he had misjudged himself and the rest of us, that it did not, in the long run, matter . . .

Of course, I did no such thing. I stood there with the rest of the officers, a prisoner of decorum as much as anything, watching as Fritzl, Stefan's batman, perched up in the driver's seat, twitched the reins and started the carriage back toward the reception at the barracks. The colonel's coach drew up and, as the best man, I rode with him, his wife, and Frau Krasinska.

"It went well, I think," I remarked, hoping that saying so might make it so, or that my unease might be private and my own irrational reaction.

"Yes, it went beautifully," Sonja replied.

"If the rest of their lives go as well, they'll have no complaint," the colonel pronounced, trying to be hearty and philosophical at the same time. He snapped open the cover of his pocket watch and looked at the time. "And it went on schedule, too."

"He is always particular about promptness," Mrs. Bergner explained, as if the colonel weren't there.

"They should be on their way by three o'clock, I'd expect," the colonel said.

"That's impressive, sir." I went along, as if it were a great achievement.

"Where are they going for their honeymoon?" the colonel's wife asked.

"Vienna," Sonja answered.

"I'm sure they'll enjoy it," the colonel's wife said.

Eugenie had very much wanted to go to Paris, but there wasn't time. Stefan had not been with the regiment long enough to have accumulated much leave. As it stood, their week in Vienna represented some generosity on the colonel's part. Eugenie had had to settle but had done so gracefully enough. Stefan had not shown much real concern one way or the other.

We arrived back at the barracks and I helped the ladies down from the carriage. The important tasks that remained for me to perform included our toast to the bride and groom and the settling of that stupid debt. I had decided that it was not a subject that could be raised before the wedding ceremony but, for Stefan's sake, it had to be disposed of before they left on their journey. I had finally resolved upon insisting that he accept his IOUs as my wedding gift. He might not be happy about it but he could not decently refuse the present or take offense at it. I was worried, though, that in the confusion he might slip away. This was not a dinner party but a more informal reception, with orderlies carrying trays of champagne and canapés and all the officers and noncoms as well as many of the important townspeople mingling cheerfully. There would be a relatively brief party and then the newlyweds would depart.

But they would need luggage, and it stood to reason that Fritzl would be the one to fetch it. I sought him out and let him know that when Stefan ordered his luggage, Fritzl was to inform me.

"Yes, sir," he promised.

"That's an order," I told him.

"I understand, sir," he said. And then added, "If I might make a suggestion, sir?"

"Yes?"

"The bride is unlikely to travel in her wedding dress. If you were to keep an eye on her, you'd have some warning. She will certainly go off to change into her traveling costume."

"Thank you," I told him. "An excellent idea. But still, when the lieutenant calls for his luggage, you let me know."

"You may depend on me, sir."

It was a sensible suggestion he'd made. The only trouble with it was that it diverted my attention from Stefan to Eugenie. I kept looking at her when I ought to have been watching him. At the colonel's signal, I proposed the first toast—"To the Emperor, and to the bride and groom!" They cut the first slice of cake together and then the chef's staff took over the cutting of the huge cake into portions. The bride and groom intertwined their arms for their first sips of champagne. They fed each other their first sweet forkfuls of cake. I drank off my champagne and turned to reach for another glass. I turned back and Stefan was gone. I saw that Eugenie was still there, standing beside her mother, drinking champagne and beaming. I had plenty of time.

But then we heard the shot. I knew immediately that it was Stefan. I knew he'd killed himself. It was as clear to me as it was to Eugenie. I saw her face change in an instant from happiness to horror and utter chagrin.

What a fool! How could he have done such a thing? How could he have done such a terrible thing to her?

XXXII · *Notes*

The commotion was very great. I told Sonja to take Eugenie home. There was nothing to be done for Stefan, of course, but for the others, we wanted to help however we could to soften the blow and diminish the pain. Someone has said that suicides are messy deaths, spattering those closest to the people who kill themselves. The aunt and uncle seemed angered. The colonel was dismayed. It was worst for Sonja and Eugenie.

Within a quarter of an hour, the reception hall was empty and the guests were dispersed. The orderlies had cleared away the glasses and stacked most of the collapsible tables except for those in the front of the room, on one of which the enormous cake still loomed, looking now for all the world like a confectionary tombstone. Some of us were sitting at the other table, guzzling from the champagne bottles on ice in the big buckets, hardly even tasting it but steadily pursuing our goal of insensibility, when Fritzl approached me.

"With the captain's permission?"

"Yes, corporal, what is it?"

"I have a note, sir. In fact, I have two of them."

"From whom?" I asked, but I knew.

"From the lieutenant. He told me to give them to you in the event that anything untoward should happen."

"And you said nothing about this to me?"

"He ordered me not to say anything, sir."

I sighed. It wasn't Fritzl's fault. "Let me have them, then." He handed me two envelopes, one addressed to Eugenie and the other with my name written on it. Both of them were unsealed.

I opened mine. Its single sheet of paper bore neither date nor salutation and its one line in Stefan's hand said, "The debt of honor is paid. Forgive me. S."

"Madman," I said, and showed my fellow officers the note.

"But what about the other note?" a lieutenant asked.

"It's addressed to his wife," I said.

"Is it sealed?"

"No, but it's addressed to her."

"I'd think he expected you to read it," a first lieutenant suggested. "Otherwise, he'd have sealed it, wouldn't he?"

"Maybe he meant to seal them both and just forgot," the second lieutenant said.

"One can't assume motives," a captain said. "When one is dealing with the dead, one can only go by what they did. And if he left it unsealed, it was presumably deliberate."

The others agreed. He'd probably thought it all out beforehand. After all, there was not likely to be an opportunity to correct mistakes later on.

"The consensus, then, is that I should at least look at what he wrote her?" I asked.

"I think so," the captain said. "You have to decide how and when and even whether to deliver it, after all."

That seemed persuasive. I opened her envelope and found the very same message, either the original or the copy. "The debt of honor is paid. Forgive me. S."

It was his way of letting her off the hook, I thought, but I said nothing. I put the letter back in its envelope, took a drink of wine, and ordered my horse. I rode out immediately to the Krasinskas to let them know what an awful misunderstanding there had been. I told her about the game of cards, Stefan's huge losses, my intention of canceling his debt. . . .

"It had nothing to do with you," I told her. "He was doing only what he thought honor demanded. It was a terrible mistake."

"Thank you for coming," Sonja said to me.

"I'm sorry. I should have spoken to him at the church," I told her.

"How could you have known?" Eugenie asked me.

I offered them my condolences and my services, if there was anything I could do for them, and I rode back to the barracks. I could see how he'd picked me to lose to, and I didn't resent having been used that way. I was even able to like him again, at least a little. Right or wrong, he'd done what he had conceived to be the necessary and honorable thing.

PART THREE

XXXIII · *A Chance Meeting*

That's where it stops.

What the captain wanted to do was to deliver these pages to Eugenie, or maybe just to send them, and then give her a few days to think about them. Once she had a chance to take it all in, he'd have popped in on her to see how she was handling it. By then, she'd be either warmer or colder, would love him or hate him and his book. And either way, he'd probably have been willing to live with her decision.

He was drawn to her. Maybe it was their both being bastards that way. Or maybe it was the way they both had odd views about life. She also was a pretty girl, which is never unimportant. But sometimes, late at night when the morphine was wearing off, he'd talk about Sonja too as if he were thinking that it might be nice to step into Stefan's shoes or, even better, bedroom slippers and nightshirt. The captain might even have been ready to go the lieutenant one better, having fond memories of Wanda from his younger days.

He was bathed in sweat, which I wiped as often as I could with a reasonably clean towel. I also found him some cool water.

"Perhaps the child will be female," he said once, laughing a little.

"Why not, sir?" I assumed he was thinking he might try for all four of them.

"For God's sake, there must be more morphine. Or brandy."

"I'll try to find some brandy for you."

"Bless you, Fritzl."

169

It wasn't such a great coincidence that we had met again, the captain and I, after our days in Waldenburg. Without the lieutenant to serve, I had been transferred to another unit, given a gun, and then, when the hostilities broke out, sent to fight. In the army, you do what you're told or they shoot you. But even if you do what they tell you, you can still get shot, which is what happened to me. Fortunately, my wound wasn't serious.

It terrified me. I thought I was dying. There was a lot of blood, and the pain was awful, but the bullet had only grazed my scalp. There was no permanent damage. Back at the field hospital, I recovered all too quickly and was assigned to the hospital transport squad, wheeling patients from place to place until they ended up with the grave detail. I also used to take supplies from one place to another when they had any for me to take. From time to time, I also helped the medical corpsmen, doing what I could for the wounded. I tried to make myself useful because it was safer in the hospital than at the front and I wanted to stay there as long as possible.

Captain Kraus had continued with the hussars, of course, but according to him, their glorious traditions had come to an end, were no longer even relevant. For all the training in horsemanship, this was a war that was being won and lost by railroad trains. Instead of generals, the captain said, there were conductors running things. He was wounded more seriously than I, and the surgeons had had to take off his left leg just above the knee. The wound had of course become infected—either from the original cannon shot or from the surgeons' own implements. The captain lay in one of the beds in the officers' ward, sometimes feverish, sometimes in terrible pain—pain that seemed to come from the part of the leg that was gone. I found him that way one night, moaning quietly and very hot. I brought him a dipper of water and as he was drinking I asked if he recognized me.

"I thought I was dreaming. It's Fritzl, isn't it?"

"Yes, sir, at your service."

"I'm not crazy, then?"

"No more than anyone else in this war."

"That's a very high standard you're setting."

"Can I get you anything else?"

"More water."

"Certainly, captain."

We were glad to see each other again, both of us survivors and from the old regiment—of which there wasn't much left. Their victory at Trautenau had cost them dearly. The estimates were that the Austrians had lost five times as many as had the Prussians they had driven from the field. Colonel Bergner was dead. Captain Kraus thought he might be the only officer to have survived. "So, you see, it's a great joke. If Stefan hadn't blown his brains out in the paddock, the Prussians would have done him the favor anyway. What's the difference?"

"I don't suppose it makes much difference now," I said, and helped him drink the fresh water.

I did what I could for him. I changed his dressings, got him to eat a little, and even fetched him broth from the kitchen late at night. There was no particular reason for what I did. It certainly wasn't generosity or kindness. Fatigue, I think, more than anything. It takes effort to harden yourself the way you have to, in such times and places, to the suffering and the dying. I had to keep myself hard all the time in order to stay there in the hospital and keep myself alive. But for Captain Kraus I let down my guard, as if to atone for all my sins. Those of that week were enough, I'm sure, to get me eternal damnation a hundred times over. If there is such a thing.

Whenever I had a moment, though, I checked on the captain, and each time I was surprised to find he was still alive. The usual route was from surgery to infection to death. I wondered why the doctors bothered. It would have been more merciful to let the poor bastards bleed to death in the first place. Quicker anyway. But Captain Kraus fought on and even recovered. His fever dropped. He asked one day for pen and paper, and I brought them. At first in brief spasms of energy that exhausted him, but then for longer periods, sometimes for entire mornings, he wrote, either in bed or, later on, outside at a camp desk under a plane tree when the weather was mild.

"You'll exhaust yourself, sir," I warned him.

"It's what keeps me alive. I live to get it all down," he told me.

"If you say so, sir."

It wasn't clear to me what he was writing. I thought at first it might be an account of his experiences in the war. When he talked, it was mostly of strategy and tactics.

"It is a whole new way of fighting, less gallant but more efficient, and much deadlier. It is funny, really, how they humiliate us. They just get on the train and go to sleep, and in the morning they are two hundred miles away. Or two hundred miles closer. To hell with the cavalry. All you need now is a timetable," he told me. So I thought he was writing mostly about the fighting.

"Benedek doesn't understand it. Nobody on the general staff does," he said. Benedek was the Austrian commander in chief, of course. "To do what the Prussians have done, they had to spread themselves very thin. They were vulnerable at almost any point. We should have realized that but we never did. Moltke assumed we wouldn't, and he was right." Moltke was the Prussian commander. "Not until Trautenau did Benedek decide to gamble, and then he learned the other great lesson."

"What lesson is that, sir?"

"With muzzle-loading rifles and sabers, you can't fight against an army that has breech-loading rifles. The Americans found that out in their civil war. It's a lesson we should have learned."

"But we won at Trautenau, sir, didn't we?"

That was when he told me what the casualties had been and laughed and couldn't stop laughing, not until he had exhausted himself. Then I helped him back to bed.

That night he explained to me he'd been writing about

172

Stefan. We were whispering, because others were trying to sleep. "I thought you were writing about the battles," I told him.

"Thinking about the battles but writing about Stefan."

"I don't see the connection."

"There isn't any."

I said nothing but looked at him oddly. He laughed and said, "It used to be that love stories were an escape from the reasonableness of life. Now that the world is crazy, love stories begin to look reasonable. It will be the new philosophy. I used to think Stefan was stupid and wrong. I'm not so sure now. He had a fairly decent death, compared to any of the hundreds we've seen this week, wouldn't you say?"

"If you look at it that way, sir, yes."

"How else can one look at it? Even worse, where else is there to look?"

I have since read that in what they call the Seven Weeks' War, the Prussian losses were 9,000 and ours were 25,000. And still, who has ever heard of Trautenau or Königgrätz?

He improved little by little and he kept asking for more and more paper. Then, on the day he announced to me that he had completed his "scribbling," the order came for him to return to Vienna.

"At last, I will have a safe little desk in the quartermaster's corps, and a wooden leg, and a quiet life. Or else . . ."

"Or else?"

"I might go back to Waldenburg. At least for a visit."

"The best of luck, sir," I said.

"You, too, Fritzl. The worst of it's over, now, I'd say. We'll make it yet."

"Thank you, sir."

He was half right. I made it. But his train was blown up. The Austrians had finally learned about moving men around on railroads, and the Prussians were ready to teach us yet another lesson—that trains are not invulnerable. There was a terrible explosion. Cars were blown off the tracks. Pieces of bodies were literally hanging in the trees.

I was assigned to go out and help with the cleaning up, and I found the small trunk, hardly scratched, on which I could read the name stenciled in dark red letters: Cptn Rudolph Kraus/5th Rgmt Hussars. I brought it back with me on a wagon loaded with corpses.

A stupid thing to do, but it was impossible to resist, for it followed upon the first stupid thing, which had been to allow myself any human feeling at all toward anyone, even a pleasant gentleman I'd known before like the captain. If there is a chink in your defenses anywhere, the gods will find it out and stick you there, twisting the knife whatever way they can.

XXXIV · *The Last Word*

Naturally, I read it.

Hard to say what I thought of it. Hard to know myself, for that matter. I had my own memories of Stefan, of the captain, and of Waldenburg. You can live in a house and hardly notice how the furniture is arranged, but then, after a flood or a fire, those little details can seem to be important, priceless. Because they are lost.

In some such way, I held on to the captain's manuscript because it was a reminder of those days in Waldenburg. Besides, who had a better claim? As far as I knew, there were no heirs to the captain's estate.

I even decided to add to it, as I've been doing in this last little piece. But then it crossed my mind that the Krasinskas were still alive. They would be interested surely. I decided that as soon as the fighting was over and I was able to get back to Waldenburg, I'd go there and take the manuscript. It wasn't any big thing, hardly an urgent mission, but it was something to think about. I wondered what they'd think and whether there might be some small reward for my trouble. You've got to live, after all, even in the midst of suffering. Especially in the midst of suffering. My work at the hospital had taught me that much.

It wasn't until late that fall that I was able to get to Waldenburg and trudge from the railroad station with the manuscript under my arm. I passed the center of the town and took the road that led to the Krasinska house. It was late in the afternoon and the day was dark anyway, with a chilly

175

kind of drizzle that kept threatening to get worse. I put my collar up around my neck, pulled my hat down over my eyes, and pressed on, mostly watching the ground before me in order to avoid puddles. It took awhile for me to notice that one of the two taverns had been burnt to the ground. The blacksmith's shop was still there but it was deserted. The church still stood, but its tower had been snapped off as if by some huge child. There had been action here, and the town had sustained some damage. It stood to reason. Why in the hell not? While the regiment had gone out to search for its fate, they could just as easily have sat back and waited. It would have come.

The bad weather covered over some of the evidence, particularly because the important things to notice were those that were missing. No cows in the fields. No horses grazing in the meadows. No pigs in the piggeries making fart smells. Just that sudden quiet one expects in a drizzle anyway, and nothing moving. I walked a little faster, anxious now, even though I knew there was nothing I could do. Whatever had happened had happened. It had come and gone. I was cold and damp and more and more convinced I'd wasted a trip, but I had to see for myself.

The walk took a half hour or maybe a little more. The house was still there. I felt a great relief. They had been spared! I would at least have some hot soup, a schnapps, and maybe a bed for the night. There was a light in back, in the kitchen window. I knocked at the side door. A stranger in his shirt sleeves looked out and asked me what I wanted.

"Is Frau Krasinska here? Or Frau F——?"

"Dead."

"Dead? Both?"

"Killed."

"And the baby?" I asked. There should have been a baby, shouldn't there?

"The old woman has it."

"Wanda?"

176

The man shrugged. He seemed to be a superior grade of servant, a butler or majordomo. "Ask at the tavern. Maybe they'll know there."

"Who owns this place now?" I asked.

"I do," the man said. "Now, get going. Or I'll set the dogs on you."

I did not dawdle. I realized on my way back that the new owner was a Prussian, one of the lucky ones the war had helped. He'd bought the place cheap and would feel annoyance at my reminder that others had been shoved aside to make room for him.

Sonja and Eugenie dead? Wanda and the baby still alive! Terrible, terrible. It was not what Stefan had expected or Captain Kraus either. It seemed to bleed out the last of whatever sense there had been in both their stories. I thought of that remark of the captain's about love stories offering a kind of sense, but he hadn't been tough enough.

It was almost dark by the time I got back to the tavern. The innkeeper told me that yes, Wanda had survived and had taken the baby—a girl.

"You know where they went?"

"Vienna, maybe. Or Budapest. Maybe Warsaw. She said she'd keep going until she found something. I don't know."

I told him a little of how the captain had kept alive, thinking of Sonja and Eugenie, but the innkeeper wasn't interested. He'd seen enough horrors to last a lifetime and didn't need anyone else's. I couldn't even get a free place to lie down in his barn. He charged me a few groschen—I think as a matter of principle.

In the morning, I drank some water from the brook and went back to the station to wait for the next train to Vienna. So much for Waldenburg, or Walbrzych, or whatever the hell it calls itself these days.

I made inquiries at the War Department in Vienna, thinking Wanda might have applied for a pension for the child. Not that she was likely to get it, but she might have tried. The lieutenant had in fact married Eugenie before he shot himself, so she qualified as a widow. In Wanda's place, I'd have tried. But I could find no record.

What then to do with the damned manuscript? Give it to Stefan's aunt and uncle? That was stupid. They'd only burn it. I could do that myself, just as easily. But what a waste!

Look, I told myself, they publish these stupid books all the time, dumb books that fill the minds of young people with all kinds of dangerous nonsense. That was what had happened to Stefan, really. He'd been influenced by writers! What about a true story, a story that told how things really are and what the world is actually going to do to you, no matter how noble or kind or sensitive you are. Let people know what life is really like! Take the fucking thing to a publisher. There could be money in it, after all.

I copied out on fresh paper the captain's manuscript and my few notes at the end and took it to one of the publishers. I sat in their waiting room, cooling my heels for an hour and then another, until finally someone came out to tell me they never read unsolicited manuscripts.

"Then what should I do with my book?"

"Write me a letter," he told me. He was a tall, almost gaunt fellow. I think he had a weak chest. I hope so.

"But I'm here," I said. "I could tell you about it. Give me five minutes."

He rolled his eyes upward as though he had borne enough misery already in one lifetime. "Two minutes," he said.

I told him about how it was a tragic love story that ended with a suicide, and yet somewhere there was a baby still alive, so that a kind of hope continued. "I have it with me," I said. "Right here."

"Let me see it."

I handed it to him. He looked at the first sentence, then read the first page. "All right," he said. "Come back in a week. I'll let you know."

I went back a week later. The receptionist had it for me. All wrapped up and tied in a ribbon. There was a note with it. I knew it was a rejection, but I opened the note.

No date. No salutation. Just the few lines: "Who could make up such a story? What kind of terrible human being could write such a novel?"

"Excuse me," I said to the receptionist. "It isn't a novel."

"I'm sorry," he said.

"It's a mistake. They don't understand. This isn't a novel. It's true," I said. "It's all true."

"I'm sorry," he said.